**Cull** good at cribbage, marching his pegs around the board in short order. Matt was pretty happy with the way he held his own too, munching chips and queso, offering Cullen the bag from time to time.

They didn't talk much, because what did they have to say? It didn't matter. He had decisions to make, and so did Cullen. He wanted to make them with a clear head, and without any influence from a desperate new owner who didn't know anything about hiring a new manager.

Cullen chuckled when Matt won the rubber. "Two out of three. Nice."

"Thanks." He stretched, surprising himself by offering to play best three out of five.

"God, yeah. Gotta give me a chance to redeem myself." Cullen laughed, the sound low and warm.

Matt dealt while Cullen moved the pegs back to the start, the act of moving the cards around settling him, letting the chatter in his brain back off. He'd missed this since Ben had passed, the simple joy of a game late at night.

Cullen was good company.

He hated to admit it, but it was true, dammit.

# Welcome to

## ⟨🌀⟩REAMSPUN DESIRES

Dear Reader,

Love is the dream. It dazzles us, makes us stronger, and brings us to our knees. Dreamspun Desires tell stories of love featuring your favorite heartwarming heroes, captivating plots, and exotic locations. Stories that make your breath catch and your imagination soar.

In the pages of these wonderful love stories, readers can escape to a world where love conquers all, the tenderness of a first kiss sweeps you away, and your heart pounds at the sight of the one you love.

When you put it all together, you find romance in its truest form.

Love always finds a way.

*Elizabeth North*

Executive Director
Dreamspinner Press

# Julia Talbot

# CATCHING HEIR

DREAMSPUN DESIRES

PUBLISHED BY

DREAMSPINNER
PRESS

Published by
DREAMSPINNER PRESS

5032 Capital Circle SW, Suite 2, PMB# 279,
Tallahassee, FL 32305-7886 USA
www.dreamspinnerpress.com

This is a work of fiction. Names, characters, places, and incidents either
are the product of author imagination or are used fictitiously, and any
resemblance to actual persons, living or dead, business establishments,
events, or locales is entirely coincidental.

Catching Heir
© 2016 Julia Talbot.

Cover Art
© 2016 Bree Archer.
http://www.breearcher.com
Cover content is for illustrative purposes only and any person depicted
on the cover is a model.

ISBN: 978-1-63477-677-6
Digital ISBN: 978-1-63477-678-3
Library of Congress Control Number: 2016913632
Published December 2016
v. 1.0

Printed in the United States of America
∞
This paper meets the requirements of
ANSI/NISO Z39.48-1992 (Permanence of Paper).

**JULIA TALBOT** lives in the great Southwest, where there is hot and cold running rodeo, cowboys, and everything from meat and potatoes to the best Tex-Mex. A full-time author, Julia has been published by Torquere Press, Dreamspinner, and Changeling Press. She believes that everyone deserves a happy ending, so she writes about love without limits, where boys love boys, girls love girls, and boys and girls get together to get wild, especially when her crazy paranormal characters are involved. Find Julia at @juliatalbot on Twitter, or at www.juliatalbot.com.

To my very own Texan, my wife, BA Tortuga.
Thank you for everything.

*Xoo Julie Talbot*

## *Chapter One*

"**THEREFORE,** Mr. Patrick, you inherit the bulk of your grandfather's estate. The portfolio is quite diverse, and I hope you will consider working with your grandfather's investment banker. I feel he's honest and walks the fine line between risk and conservancy."

Cullen Patrick nodded slowly, his brain hurting from all the information he'd absorbed in the last hour. His Grandpa Patrick, who he didn't even remember, was dead. He'd been a rich old dude, and now Cullen was a rich early-thirties dude. With a varied portfolio. The one thing he did remember, however, wasn't in the paperwork.

"What about the Treeline?" Cullen asked, referring to the hotel his dad had talked about his whole life.

Cullen had never stayed there or been to see his grandpa, but he'd seen pictures and stuff and had always loved the look of the stately Victorian-era hotel in Colorado.

"Ah, yes. Well, I saved that for last, as the arrangements are very complicated." Mr. Rollins, the lawyer, smiled, and Cullen stared.

He was pooped. They'd found him in Grenoble, working the slopes like a fiend to get ready for Oslo. Then he'd flown first class to Denver and had a car pick him up and take him out to somewhere outside of Aspen. The X Games were in Aspen, so he knew the area, but he'd never allowed himself to go see the Treeline.

"Complicated how?" Cullen finally asked.

"Your grandfather intended to bequeath the Treeline to Matt Nathanson, the current general manager, but felt strongly that the family ties that existed should be respected. Ergo, the hotel is owned by you, but Mr. Nathanson's position is to be retained, his retirement benefits assured, and all modifications to the hotel must meet with his approval."

"His approval…." Weird. "Is this Matt guy super old or something?"

"No. No, in fact I believe he's a year or two younger than you, Mr. Patrick."

"No shit." It popped out and Cullen chuckled. "Pardon my French. So, what's his deal?"

"Pardon me? What deal?"

"This Matthew guy. I mean, why would the old man want him to have a lifetime job? Boy toy? Illegitimate heir? Something out of a horror movie?" He warmed to his theme, thinking very Stephen King shit.

"He took care of your grandfather for the past ten years, even when things were… unpleasant." The lawyer's nose wrinkled, and Cullen could only imagine what that meant.

Unpleasant.

How entertaining. Maybe gore wasn't necessary when you had old-guy smell.

Cullen was suddenly grateful his dad had gone so fast, the cancer diagnosed too late to do more than put him in hospice. Boom. Too young to go or not, it had to be better than lingering until you were ninety and sitting in your own mess all day. "Does this guy live at the hotel?"

"He does. He has an apartment on the second floor, above the lobby."

"Wow. This guy is dedicated." Okay, so he owned the hotel, but he had to share it? Maybe he could buy this Matthew guy out or something. Of course, if he was a good manager and his salary was in a trust and stuff, maybe he could just stay. "What else do I need to know?"

"That's really it. There are approximately a zillion pieces of paper for you to sign, but that's it."

Cullen chuckled, the more relaxed lawyer way more his style. "Do I have the money guy's number?"

"Would you like my assistant to make you an appointment?"

"I would." That was too cool. Oh, he had sponsors who made arrangements for him and shit, but Cullen was still used to picking up his cell and calling people.

"Excellent. We'll arrange everything. Will you be in the area for a while?"

"I think so, yeah." He thought he might skip Oslo and train up for Aspen....

"Well, leave your contact information with me, and we'll have everything arranged."

"Good deal. Let's push paper."

An hour later, he'd signed those zillion papers and maybe a few hundred more. He shook out his left hand, which was cramped into a permanent claw.

"Can I go stay at the hotel? Do I need to make a reservation or anything?" He had no idea what to do. Hell, he'd missed the funeral by, like, two weeks.

"It's under a bit of renovation, but it is yours, after all. I'll call and let Matt know you're coming."

"Thanks." Grandpa Patrick had to have some kind of living quarters there. The house in Basalt was… sort of sterile and unlived-in. Like a vacation rental from yesteryear.

He'd have to find someone who wanted to rent it out, maybe do a swap. He loved that shit. Cullen would bet some of his buddies in Chamonix or Sestriere would switch with him.

"I appreciate all your help," Cullen said, standing and holding out a hand to shake. "I'm sorry I never got to meet him. Grandpa. Dad was… opposed."

"Yes. Family dynamics are challenging, aren't they?"

"They sure were with Dad. He had feels." He grinned when all he got was a blank stare. Yeah, his slang was five, ten years younger than he was, even. Snowboarders were a hoot that way. "I think I'm going to find the Treeline and flop for a while. Holler at me if I need to sign anything else."

"I can do that. Have a good afternoon."

"Thanks again."

His driver leaped up when Cullen left the lawyer's inner sanctum, and Cullen chuckled. "Are you on my payroll or this guy's?"

"Until I drop you off, that guy's. Do you need a driver on your payroll? I'm available."

Oh, he liked that. Not that he couldn't drive, but he would have a lot of people to ferry back and forth. "Yeah. Submit a salary proposal, and I'll see what's in my new budget."

"You have a card?" There was a tick; then the dude grinned. "Sir."

"I do!" He pulled out his card, which had *X Games champion* scrolled under his name. He wrote his cell number on it. Then his e-mail. "Just e-mail me your thing."

"I'm all over it. I watched you in Salt Lake. You rocked it."

"Thanks." He put his hand up for a high five and got it. Rock on. "Are you up to taking me out to the Treeline Hotel?"

"Sure. Wherever you want. I'm yours for the afternoon."

"Woo! I'll buy you a beer when we get there." If the bar was open during the renovation. Hell, if not, there had to be a Kum & Go or something.

"It's a fair deal. Let's go, man. It's a killer drive up the mountain."

Oh, most excellent. He was all over that shit. He might have to get his motorcycle here and do the drive on it, but today he could just look, really enjoy the view. This guy…. "What's your name?"

"Brandon. Brandon Harris."

"Nice to meet you, Brandon." Today he could let Brandon drive him, and he could see what there was to see.

The rest of the stuff he would deal with as he came to it.

## Chapter Two

**THE** phone was ringing off the hook, and Matt answered a call as he ran down the stairs to see what the issue with the plumbing was now. "Good evening. Treeline Estates. How may I direct your call?"

God help him, but Belinda was off on maternity leave during the renovations, and while that timing was great, he hadn't realized how many phone calls a day he'd be fielding.

"I'd like to make a reservation for December, please."

"Of course, sir. Give me one second to get into that screen." Thank God for tablets, Wi-Fi, and POS systems. He took the reservation while glaring at one of the little subcontractors and texting Neville, the general contractor, all at the same time. "How many guests?"

The man reserved two rooms in the east tower, which was almost finished, thank God. The subcontractor's phone rang, and Matt heard Neville screaming when the guy answered.

"Fix it," he snapped, then headed to check on Jeanette and make sure the new housekeeping storage and laundry facilities were functional. His phone rang again. "Treeline Estates, can I help you?"

"Boss. Geoff. Someone's pulling up the drive in a limo."

"We don't have any guests booked, Geoff. They must be lost."

"Doesn't look like it. Professional driver. Local guy. VIP something, from the looks."

"Oh, for…." *Peace. Peace and ease. Peace, ease, and Zen. Peace, ease, Zen, and a huge hammer.* "Stall them, and I'll check the logs."

He checked for reservations, but he was at occupancy zero. Okay. Okay, good. Next he called Jeanette. "Hey, lady. Is there a VIP suite that can be made ready in case someone's fucked up and booked the room?"

"Yes, sir. The Presidential is still being painted, but the Patrick suite is ready."

"Excellent. Can you call Devlin and tell him that there's a chance he'll be feeding a guest en suite tonight? I'll know more in ten."

"I'll do that right now." She hung up, and Matt breathed deeply again, smelling paint, which had been the order of the day since the work began.

Neville called as he jogged upstairs. "It's an easy fix. He'll have it done in twenty minutes, no worries."

"I sure hope so, Nev. I have a VIP guest who just showed up. I don't need this shit." He and Neville understood each other. They were both transplanted Texans.

"You have my word. I thought you were empty, you know?"

"So did I." Another call buzzed in. Geoff. "Gotta go, Nev. Geoff?"

"Says he's the new owner, boss. Like, for reals. That he's Mr. Patrick."

Matt stopped, damn near going ass over teakettle. "What?"

"Maybe a few years older than you. Blond. Blue eyes. ID says Cullen Patrick, Park City, Utah."

"Okay. Okay. Uh." Shit. Shit. Shit. "Have the driver stay. Show Mr. Patrick to the sitting room, and I'll be there shortly." *After I kill someone.* He dialed Mr. Rollins, Esq., snarling when Jody answered the phone. "This is Matt Nathanson. Get me Rollins. Right now."

"Yes, sir. Of course."

The fact that she immediately agreed set all his "you've been fucked" meters ringing, and he worked in the hotel business. His were set on incredibly low sensitivity.

"Matt. How's it going out there?" Rollins put on his feeble old man voice. Always a bad sign.

"Don't. Who is this rolling up to the lobby and saying that he's the new owner, and why the hell didn't I get any warning?" It was bad enough that Ben's family had deserted him and left him for strangers to care for and love, but now this? Suddenly there was money, and he had a new fucking boss? That wasn't supposed to be the deal. He didn't want Ben's cash. He wanted the Treeline. He'd given Ben and this place his life for more than a decade. He'd earned his place here.

"Matt, please. I didn't have time to call. He just left my office, and I had a conference call right after. I had no idea we'd actually tracked down Ben's grandson until he showed up today. A junior partner was doing the legwork."

Matt stopped on the landing, plopped down on his ass, and closed his eyes. It wasn't a joke. It wasn't a lie. "I'll go upstairs and pack my shit. Tell the new guy good luck with Nev."

Matt hoped Nev ass fucked the new guy and left him broke and blind.

"Oh, do stop being melodramatic, Matthew. The Treeline trust provides very well for you, and for your position. You knew this might happen. Buck up and fight for your place."

"My place." No. No, it wasn't his. He'd thought it was going to be, but it wasn't. He was an employee. Just another hotel manager.

"Yes. It is. I tried to get Ben to change his will, Matt. By the time he finally decided to, it was too late. We had an appointment the day after he died. Perhaps I shouldn't tell you, but you need to know. He wanted you to have the hotel."

"That's great. I'm tickled." Whatever. Christ, he wanted to lay down and die. He'd believed…. Shit. He really had thought for a few weeks that this pipe dream was real.

"Don't give up, Matt. Promise me you'll wait for a bit before you make any decisions."

His phone beeped; yet another call coming in.

"I have to go. Someone's calling." He hung up, then clicked over. "Treeline Estates, how can I help you?"

"Boss, I need you." Geoff again, calling from a cell. "He wants to see you."

"I'm coming. He can freaking wait until I fucking get there." He didn't work for the son of a bitch; the asshole could chill his heels.

"Okay." Geoff sounded taken aback, and why shouldn't he? Matt leaped to assist any guest.

"I'll be there in five, okay?" He hung up, then dropped his head in his hands. *Peace. Peace and Zen, and a big motherfucking rock.*

He finally made his way downstairs, steeling himself to meet Ben's grandson, who had never even met the old man. Not once.

He didn't work for this man. He didn't answer to the son of a bitch. He didn't give a fuck.

Hell, he didn't give half a fuck.

The guy waiting for him at the front desk looked like a snow bunny crossed with—Matt would have called it "Austin hipster," but Geoff had said Utah. Jeans, boots, a Jeep Naked sweatshirt, and rough chopped gold hair that grew just below chin length.

"Mr. Patrick? I'm Mr. Nathanson. Pleased to meet you." He put on his best "hey, you're an asshole, and I have to deal with you" face.

"Hey." Patrick held out a hand. "Cullen. I was hoping I could stay a few days despite the reno."

"We aren't really open right now, I'm afraid. It's another six weeks, tops, before we start accepting guests." *You assmonkey.*

"Oh, Geoff here already told me the Patrick suite was okay. My namesake and all." Cullen Patrick grinned at him, looking cheerful, but those blue eyes were watchful, just as Ben's had been.

He shot Geoff a look. "Well, obviously the valet has his finger on the pulse of what's going on."

And was so fucking fired.

Geoff sighed, shoulders slumping, clearly reacting to his mood.

"Hey, I don't want to be a drag. Did Grandpa have an apartment or anything? I could stay there instead. It's just a long way back to Basalt."

"No. I'll have the room checked, and then someone will come for you. Have a seat. Geoff, can you please fetch Mr. Patrick's luggage?"

"Yes, sir." Geoff hopped to it.

"I'm sure you're super busy, but maybe I could talk with you over supper or something?" Cullen asked. "I wanted to chat with you about the terms of the will and the hotel and all."

"Of course." Goody, he couldn't fucking wait. "I'll speak to the chef and have him arrange something. The restaurant isn't open, of course, but if you'll let me know your preferences...."

"Oh, I can eat anything proteiny. I love omelets and shit. Turkey burgers. Fish is good. If I wasn't coming up so hard on the grand prix, I would beg for a barbecue burger. The lawyer didn't tell me a whole lot, so I bet he didn't let you know I was coming."

"Indeed. You might even say we didn't know you existed." The phone rang and he jumped. "If you'll excuse me. Treeline Estates, how can I help you? No, I'm sorry. We are already fully booked for the holidays. I do have a waiting list, if you'd prefer?"

He headed out, texting Devlin.

*VIP, protein, in-room dining.*

All he had to do was work right now. He could think and have his meltdown—and fire Geoff—later.

**AFTER** spending an hour or two sitting on his ass, Cullen headed out to explore his hotel. Because it was his, dammit, and he didn't need to feel like a guest, right? Oh, he had no urge to order people around, but he was pretty… irked at how summarily he'd been dismissed by Nathanson, the manager.

The guy was young, a tall, dark guy with an air of stodgy around him. No wonder his grandfather appreciated the dude. One stuffed shirt plumping up another.

The lobby looked pretty good. Fresh paint. New upholstery on the massive sofas. The paintings had been cleaned, which he knew thanks to a short-lived art history minor he'd taken due to Hayden of the amazing blow job, who was an art history major.

Once you got beyond the lobby, though? Man, that shit was rough. The place was clean enough, but Jesus Christ, look at how everything was worn. The carpet on the main stairs, for instance, had runners in it, the green faded, the florals muddy. There had been a leak in the second-floor hallway, badly patched and yellowing.

The whole place seemed as if it had been washed one too many times.

Cullen peered into a couple of display cases in the hallway. All of his ancestors lined up and playing croquet. Lord.

How uptight and old and just…. Why didn't anything get updated? Why was it all so fucking ancient? This guy Nathanson was supposed to be all passionate about the hotel.

"Hey." He grabbed a passing guy in uniform. "What's with the leak?"

"Pardon me?" The dude gave him a wide-eyed stare.

"Sorry. I'm Mr. Patrick's grandson. I've been wandering. What happened there?" He dragged the kid over and pointed.

"There was a broken pipe that had to be repaired."

"But why is it still obvious it was there? Does the manager guy not do his job?" Cullen knew he was being an ass, but he was a little pissy at the way Nathanson had just put him off.

"I've got this, Peter." An older woman stepped up, held out one hand, "Yvonne. Pleased."

"Nice to meet you." Cullen glanced at her name tag, trying not to be obvious. It read *Group Sales.* "Cullen Patrick."

"Are you a Cullen or a Mr. Patrick?"

"Cullen, for sure." No one ever called him Mr.

"Cullen, let's have a little tour and chat."

"What happened with the leak?"

"Mr. Nathanson repaired it."

"But not the ceiling? I mean, it's cosmetic, I realize, but these things make the place look sad."

"He repaired the ceiling as best he could with our limitations at the time. Plaster work is such a delicate thing."

"Is carpet?" He waved a hand at the frayed stairs.

"Well, yes." She smiled faintly. "The carpets here are a custom pattern created just for us by a mill in the Carolinas. They take time and money to replace."

"So, what? He's just hoarding it?"

He got an utterly confused look. "Hoarding what?"

"My grandpa's money!" Cullen flapped a hand. "I mean, the old man was loaded. Why isn't the money going back into the hotel?"

"It is now." Her tone was polite but not the warmest ever.

"What does that mean?" Cullen stared, waiting. He could do cold and concise too.

"It means that the trust was formed after Mr. Patrick passed away. Until then, Mr. Patrick decided the budget for any repairs."

"So wait, you mean to tell me Grandpa Patrick was a stingy pants? My dad always said this hotel was his whole life."

"I mean to tell you that Mr. Patrick was very ill and had some... cognitive difficulties."

"Huh." He pondered that. "So what about Nathanson? Is he a good boss?"

"Matt is an exceptional manager, fair and reasonable. I'd work for him anywhere."

Wow. He thought she meant it too. Ouch. No one wanted to hear that their family member was a nutball at the end. "Thanks. Sorry if I upset you." He was gonna go grill the valet next.

"Not at all. Let me give you the tour."

"I appreciate it. Group sales, huh? If I wanted to book some rooms for a bunch of snowboarders on a tour that would be you, then?"

"That would absolutely be me. Come on, I'll show you the ballroom. It's going to be spectacular."

"Is that part of the renovation?"

"It's part of stage one," she told him. "The first-floor rooms, the main patron areas, and the ballroom roll out in a month."

"He's doing a lot of work, right?"

"He is." She led him back downstairs, then to a set of immense double doors off the lobby.

The ballroom was in disarray, but he could see the work happening, see the exceptional bones. The place had a Gilded Age sort of decadence that needed coaxing back out, but man, it would be sweet when it was done. "What all will people do with this room. Like weddings?"

"Weddings, parties. I think we should have a fabulous Halloween ball next year. A masquerade!"

"That sounds awesome." She seemed so enthused, and fuck knew Cullen was used to cheering people on, coming from the sporting world.

"Doesn't it? There are so many of the historical registry committee people who want to see this place back to its former glory."

"I bet." Cullen felt utterly puzzled. All the stories of his youth told him his grandpa loved the hotel more than he had his son. Why wouldn't he spend the money to keep the place in fine form?

He didn't get it. He had the sinking suspicion he wouldn't be getting a lot of information from Nathanson, either. That man was a cold fish. Like tuna on ice. Buttoned up tighter than a cholo's collar.

Cullen snorted at that one. He'd have to remember it when he went to LA to skateboard with his buddy Easy next spring.

"Tell me about this historical society thingy." Maybe someone there would have some insight on what was really happening around here. Someone not on the payroll.

"The building is registered, and the people on the committee have many opinions about Matt's renovation ideas. He's been very patient with them."

"Yeah? He doesn't seem the, uh, waiting kind." Nathanson seemed the brush-off kind.

"I'm sorry? I don't follow."

"Well, he didn't strike me as a guy who wanted input." Cullen shrugged. "Granted, I met him for, like, a minute, but he made it clear he didn't have the time to chat."

"He's incredibly busy. He's been trying so hard to work the restoration and... well, no one expected you, and only days before the hotel ownership would transfer. I'm sure that's a shock, to go from owner to employee in minutes."

"He wasn't ever the owner."

"No. No, I suppose he wasn't."

He could tell she was getting uncomfortable, but he couldn't just let it stand. And what did that mean, just days before the transfer? *Mental note: Call the damned lawyer.*

The last fucking thing he needed was an employee that he couldn't fire.

Cullen held the rest of his opinions back during the tour, but by the time he was ready to go meet Nathanson for supper he was loaded for bear with a list of shit he wanted to gnaw on the man about.

He headed to the lobby, not sure exactly where he was supposed to meet Mr. Stick Up His Ass.

Man, he wasn't this way. Cullen prided himself on his easy disposition, on his ability to shrug off stress. Life was too short to be like his grandpa, right? *Shake it off, man.*

"Mr. Patrick?" A plump older woman walked up to him, all smiles. "Matt's dealing with a plumbing issue and asked me to find you and make sure you have a lovely supper."

"He's not coming?" Didn't the guy know how to delegate?

"I believe his exact words were, 'Tell him I'd be happy to show, but I'm up to my ass in alligators and am in the midst of a shitstorm.'"

Cullen blinked. "A shitstorm, huh? Sounds less yay than supper. I'll opt for the food."

"Indeed. Chef says he has a lovely omelet meal for you. Would you prefer it delivered to your room?"

"Yeah. I think it's time to go lick the proverbial wounds."

Her eyebrows rose, but he turned on his heel and headed back to his room. Maybe he should call… uh, the driver guy. He could go back to Basalt. Then again, that smacked of running away, and he wasn't a coward. Pissed off, sure, but not scared.

The food came only minutes later, and he had to admit it was filling and fucking delicious. He didn't expect eggs to be so damned good, but this was similar to the omelets he got in Italy. Prosciutto and salty cheese with this crisp salad on the side.

Yum.

He ate it all, and then let himself eat the amazing croissant that came with. Tomorrow he would get out and run a few miles or something. Or hell, check out the fitness center here. If he was going to get the tour to stay here, it needed to be state-of-the-art.

Wouldn't that rock? To get all his buddies here? They would love it. The guys would love it even more if there were some private cabins, maybe with hot tubs. Hmm.

Maybe he ought to involve himself a little bit. He could make this place what he wanted and still leave the historical stuff intact. There was plenty of land, right? Maybe see about putting in a winter park.

Somewhere to train, somewhere fun and young and not... stodgy.

Cullen grinned, lifting the last lid on the tray to find a mile-high piece of carrot cake. He moaned. Okay, he'd run a lot of miles. This was worth it.

The only way it would be better would be if someone was there to share it. Someone naked and wanting. God, he was horny. Carrot cake shouldn't be an aphrodisiac, but he ate sweets so rarely.... Maybe he'd save it for, like, 3:00 a.m., when he was so lonely he couldn't bear it.

This was why Cullen usually rented a condo or chalet with a bunch of the guys. There was always noise and something or someone to do.

Not this horrible... deadness.

He put the dome back and wandered to the settee across from the bed. He turned on the TV, the cheerful canned laughter of some sitcom easing the huge noise in his head. He was a professional athlete for a reason.

Cullen hated to be alone.

## *Chapter Three*

**HOLY** shit, Matt was starving. He had dealt with
every emergency known to man, every stupid fucking
phone call, and the fact that he had a guest in the
Patrick suite.

He hadn't fired Geoff, but the man knew the deep
shit he was in.

Matt dug out some cream cheese and some crackers,
then grabbed a bowl of chile con queso to pop in the
microwave.

The big kitchen echoed with emptiness, everyone
else gone for the night. Matt lived for times like this,
when he could breathe, no fires to put out.

He started munching, nibbling his way through the
crackers as he waited for the queso to heat up. He loved
Dev's queso dip.

This whole situation sucked, and he wished Ben were here, just to talk to, to sit and play chess and drink the dark rich coffee he loved. He missed Ben so badly it hurt. Now Matt felt as though he was just wandering in a haunted house sometimes.

He wanted to make this place something wonderful, something Ben would have loved in another life.

A slight scrape of a shoe on the floor behind him made him whirl around, afraid he'd conjured up Ben's ghost with his wistful thoughts.

"Shit!" Matt came face-to-face with, not a ghost, but with Cullen Patrick, Ben's grandson. "Sorry. Sorry, I didn't mean to—whatever."

*Please go away. Just leave me alone.* Matt closed his eyes, his heart pounding.

"I—is there any more carrot cake?" Cullen stepped into the light, his *Star Wars* pajama pants and pale blue T-shirt making him look like a teenager.

"I'm sure there is. Give me a minute, and I'll get you a piece." Carrot cake. Okay. That would be in the walk-in. He grabbed a plate and then went on a hunt for the cake.

There it was. He went ahead and cut two pieces because the big cake looked stunning. He'd have it after queso.

"Here you go," Matt said, summoning what he hoped was a smile.

"Thanks." Cullen took the plate, then stood there, shifting from foot to foot.

"Do you need anything else?" His queso beeped.

"No. I mean…." Cullen sighed. "You don't want me around at all, I know, but can I sit with you just a minute?"

"Sure. Have a seat." Goddammit. He was too fucking on edge for this shit. Still, he put on his management face because that was his job. "Do you want anything to drink?"

"Oh, just point me toward the milk." Cullen smiled a bit, but the lines around his eyes and mouth said he was tired.

"There are cartons here." He opened the fridge and pulled two out, handing them both over before putting the cream cheese back. He should have stayed in his quarters. He had cereal and Pop-Tarts up there.

"Thanks." Cullen pulled a stool up to the counter, and thankfully he didn't chatter. In fact, he was very self-contained.

Matt stirred his queso, put it back in, finished his Coke.

Cullen glanced at him every so often, and Matt could feel the curiosity, the questions trying to get out. He guessed he was supposed to help, but he didn't really want to. It wasn't his job. Well, okay, technically it was, but he was off-duty, right?

"Look, can I ask you something straight-out?" Cullen finally said after licking icing off his fork.

"Of course." Didn't mean he'd answer it, but whatever.

"Was my granddad really that tight? With the money for the hotel, I mean."

"He was ill." Ben hadn't seen the problems, had believed they were lying to him, trying to steal from him. It had been easier to let the hotel slip than to see an old man believe that the people he loved were betraying him.

"What does that mean?" Cullen leaned his elbows on the island, staring at him intently. "I mean, my dad had cancer, you know? He was sick, but it happened pretty quick. Did Grandpa have Alzheimer's? Dementia? Liver toxicity?"

Matt would have snapped, but Cullen didn't appear to be flip, really. "He was very paranoid, and he had dementia. He didn't see what we saw. He believed the hotel looked as it did in the fifties."

"Oh, wow." Cullen seemed to mull that over. "That had to be rough."

"It was. He was very confused, and we wanted to make him as happy as we could."

"Was he? Happy?"

Cullen watched him carefully, the whole pleasant "dude" demeanor fallen away.

"No. No, not for the last five years. He was angry and scared. His last two weeks, though, were very good. We had a lot of time together then. He was a chess fanatic, and we played for hours." Somehow it eased something in Matt to be able to talk about Ben, to not have to defend him or condemn him.

"I'm glad he was better at the end, then." Cullen grimaced. "Dad was a bear. He got chemical craziness from the drugs they had him on, you know? Screamed a lot. Hit the hospice nurse. It was a mess."

"Your grandfather had a nurse, but only for a few days. We managed his care for the most part."

"We?" Cullen tilted his head. "Does that mean you?"

"Yes." It had been his honor.

"That's a lot to take on." Cullen nodded, looking almost as if he'd made some sort of decision. "Thank you. I mean, I know I didn't know him, but thank you anyway."

"It was the right thing to do." He'd loved Ben as if the man had been his own grandfather, so he'd done the hard work.

"Yeah." Cullen sighed and rose, turning in a circle with his plate and glass. "I guess there's not, like, a regular dishwasher. Can I just do these in the sink?"

"I'll take care of them. Don't worry about it."

"Hey, I can do dishes." Cullen flashed him a smile he'd bet was practiced for cameras. "Seriously."

"I'll have to do mine anyway, assuming I haven't let everything go to glue."

"Okay, sure." Cullen sighed. "It's not always this quiet, is it?" He looked resigned, maybe. Possibly apprehensive?

"Lord no. We're just closed for renovations. I'm completely booked for weeks after we reopen. Everyone's excited to see the new place."

"Cool. I'm just—" Cullen laughed, a sharp bark of sound. "I should let you get back to your time off. Sorry. Night."

"Are you okay?" He shouldn't care, but that was why he was here, wasn't it? Because he cared about his guests' comfort.

"It's stupid. I've been on tour almost constantly since I was fourteen. I just don't know how to be alone, I guess. I think you might be the opposite. You need your time away."

"Ah. Well, any place that is meant to hold hundreds of people must seem weird when it's empty, huh?" He sort of got that.

"Yeah. I mean, the condo would be worse. At least here I can harass your night auditor."

He didn't know how to respond to that. What was he supposed to say? He wasn't completely sure he was going to stay at all, and he absolutely wasn't going to make friends with Mr. Patrick.

"So, yeah. Night." Cullen set the dishes on the counter and headed out, shoulders hunched. What a strange combination of men Cullen Patrick seemed to be. Super dude and vulnerable kid.

Still, he could no more let the man walk off than he could rest knowing a guest was miserable. "Do you play cribbage?"

"Yeah." Cullen turned back to face him. "I do, actually."

"There's a board in the break room back here."

"That would rock. Prepare to go down in flames."

Matt rolled his eyes. Ah, this was Ben's grandson, no doubt. "I don't have to brag, buddy. My play will speak for itself." Matt led the way into the break room. What could it hurt?

Maybe this would be a fitting end. Full circle.

Matt didn't let himself wonder where he would go now. Hotels always needed managers. Maybe Boulder. Or Glenwood. Glenwood was hot now. Growing. Hell, Glenwood Springs and Carbondale had a ton of historic buildings that could be hotels. If he got a decent severance deal for giving up his interest in the Treeline….

"You're scowling." Cullen stared at him curiously. "Seriously, you don't have to do this. It's super nice of you and all, but I can figure out something."

"Am I? I was just thinking. Have a seat. I'll grab the cards and my food."

"Cool." Cullen plopped down and set up the board after he laid it out, plugged little pegs into starting holes.

He grabbed his queso and some tortilla chips and another Coke and brought it to the table. Matt settled in, handing the deck of cards to Cullen. He was starving.

"Smells good," Cullen murmured.

"It is." Spicy and creamy and right.

"I just powered down two pieces of carrot cake. How can I still be hungry?"

"Stress," Matt said promptly. He knew all about that.

"Yeah. Do you have a fitness room?"

"No. No, I was considering putting one in, but it's not what our customers ask for."

"I guess not." Cullen chewed his lower lip. "Is there a hiking trail or anything?" He dealt out six cards to each of them.

"Oh, absolutely. The grounds are amazing. We…. You own a huge parcel of land."

"Cool. I have some stuff to talk to you about, but I think we can be on the click first, you know?" Cullen tossed two cards into the crib pile.

No, actually he didn't know, but he was an expert at playing along until he figured it out. He pulled out two cards as well, hoping he was leaving Cullen dick to use for points. That wasn't personal. He hated losing at cards.

He'd lost enough today.

Cullen turned out to be damned good at cribbage, marching his pegs around the board in short order. Matt was pretty happy with the way he held his own too, munching chips and queso, offering Cullen the bag from time to time.

They didn't talk much, because what did they have to say? It didn't matter. He had decisions to make, and so did Cullen. He wanted to make them with a clear head, and without any influence from a desperate new owner who didn't know anything about hiring a new manager.

Cullen chuckled when Matt won the rubber. "Two out of three. Nice."

"Thanks." He stretched, surprising himself by offering to play best three out of five.

"God, yeah. Gotta give me a chance to redeem myself." Cullen laughed, the sound low and warm.

Matt dealt while Cullen moved the pegs back to the start, the act of moving the cards around settling him, letting the chatter in his brain back off. He'd missed this since Ben had passed, the simple joy of a game late at night.

Cullen was good company.

He hated to admit it, but it was true, dammit.

"You okay?" The guy was also way more observant than the snowboarder-dude persona he'd put on made one believe.

"Just have a lot of decisions to make. Nothing for you to stress."

"Oh, I don't know. If you quit, I'm in trouble." Cullen chuckled. "I read all the paperwork. I may own the place, but you're pretty autonomous as far as the hotel is concerned."

"Yes, well...." He gave Cullen what he hoped was a casual shrug. "The situation has changed."

"So did I miss something? Someone today said something about a waiting period almost being over, but the lawyer never mentioned that."

"Ben left the Treeline in trust. It transferred to my ownership twenty-four months after his death, assuming no family members were found." Matt wasn't this big greedy bastard, was he? He'd just begun to believe that the fantasy was going to come true. "Since you were, the property remains in trust in perpetuity."

"Yeah, and that trust provides for your position permanently." Cullen studied his cards. "I'm not a jerk, okay. I get it. Well, I guess I don't, but I can see where it would suck for you. I just hope you won't do anything too spur of the moment."

"Yeah." And it really wasn't Cullen's business if he wanted to be more than an employee, was it? Someone like Cullen only had people working for him. It was similar to trying to explain something to Ben. They weren't in the same class, and if Matt had learned anything, it was that even Ben, who'd cared for him, believed that he was really only good enough to be a trusted employee.

Shit, that was depressing.

"Tell me to stop eating, huh? I'll have to run ten miles tomorrow."

"Yeah?" He didn't stress it. He had the metabolism of an eight-year-old. "There are trails."

"You said. I know you said customers aren't into a fitness center, but there's plenty of land here to put in a spa kind of deal."

"There's lots of space." But that wasn't what the Treeline had been.

"Yeah. I mean, I can totally see preserving the old hotel as it is, only, like, fancy again. Then taking some space where it won't impede the view and making some modern stuff. Best of both worlds." Cullen waved a chip in the air enthusiastically.

Matt smiled at Cullen, listening with half an ear and a sinking feeling in his heart. Fuck, he hated this shit.

He loved this old hotel, though.

Cullen lost the next game, then pushed away from the table, quietly cleaning up his plate. "I think I've taken up enough of your time, dude. Thanks for keeping me company."

"You're welcome." He took his dishes and started the hot water up, mind filling up with the eighty thousand things that he needed to do tomorrow.

"Night." Cullen slid out of the room, disappearing like a ghost.

"Night." He stared at the wall, listening to the water run. Matt wanted to go back to this morning. That wasn't happening. No, so he needed to pull up his socks.

He needed to get some sleep, focus, and just make rational decisions, right?

Right.

Too bad that was easier said than done.

CULLEN waited until 9:00 a.m. to call the lawyer. That was a tough thing to do, because he didn't sleep all damned night. He had wandered the empty halls of the hotel, he'd run the stairs, and he'd played wall ball down in the basement level.

He was exhausted from reading riders to the will, and he wanted to make sure he understood everything as well as vent his spleen just a teeny bit for the guy not telling him about the year after death clause or whatever.

"Good morning, Mr. Rollins's office. This is Jody. How may I help you?" Wow, she was perky.

"Hi, this is Cullen Patrick. I need to speak to Mr. Rollins."

"Yes, of course. Can I put you on hold, please?"

"Sure." He tapped his pencil on the table. He'd grabbed that and a legal pad in case he needed to take notes.

Rollins's voice was all gravel and smoke. "Mr. Patrick? How can I help you?"

"Hey." He tried to get his thoughts going downhill, not moguls. "I need to talk to you about the hotel. Did Matt Nathanson really stand to inherit fully this week?"

"He did. The day after tomorrow, in fact."

Like it was no big deal. Just screw with a dude's life. Boom.

"Why didn't you tell me, man? I would have handled this a lot differently." Cullen knew he could be a bulldozer, but, dude.

"It honestly didn't occur to me. You are here, so the situation doesn't exist."

"Yeah, but it gives me a whole different perspective on him being such a dick."

"He's always been a very decent man, in my experience."

Yeah, well. Cullen was getting tired of hearing it. Oh, Matt had been real nice last night. Really. Cullen knew it had to chafe for Matt to have him all up in his business. Still, decent and kind couldn't hide the fact that Matt hated him for existing.

"Anything else I need to know? And I mean anything, not just what you think is important."

"The trust is straightforward. Matt cannot be terminated, and all managerial decisions must have his approval. He receives a salary plus a certain percentage of profit sharing, along with his rooms. The actual property is yours fully if he resigns."

"Right, but the money in the trust still goes toward the hotel maintenance?" He'd read it over and over, and he was still a little shaky. "I mean, I'm pretty sure him resigning now would suck, but that seems the direction he's leaning."

"That would be a mistake. I'll speak to him again. He won't find another deal as secure."

"Thanks." Maybe it was crazy to try to keep Matt on with the baggage that came attached, but Cullen really had very little interest in running the hotel itself. Let Matt deal with that headache. He wanted more of a winter wonderland.

He wanted somewhere to chill the fuck out and play. To goof off and have a beer and a steak.

The two could coexist. They could even thrive if Cullen could get Matt on board.

"Anyway," Cullen went on. "Can you remind me of the name of the financial guy? I need to talk about some investments."

"Jody has a call into Dirk for an appointment for you. Dirk Bones. Can you believe the name?"

Was that a joke? "Wow." That was all Cullen could come up with. "Thanks. She'll call me?"

"Yes, sir. As soon as she has information."

"Good deal." Cullen guessed that was that, even if the conversation hadn't told him shit. "Thank you, Mr. Rollins."

They hung up, and Cullen sat there, staring at the doodles he'd drawn while on the phone. Snowcapped mountains. They were always what he drew, sometimes with a ski lift or a yeti. Today it was an avalanche.

It didn't take a psychologist to read that.

He sighed and tried to decide whether to call for oatmeal or just go to bed. His head was starting to pound, his eyes dry and heavy.

Fuck it, he'd just sleep. Maybe take a melatonin.

Oh God, he wanted a fucking joint. Damn drug tests. Once the season was over…. He'd be thinking about next season. Cullen sighed and stripped off, heading for the shower. Hopefully the water was hot.

The suite was damn amazing, and he wondered where his grandfather had slept, where Matt had kept the old man. That wasn't fair, was it? Grandpa had been his own man until he got sick. From what Cullen's dad had said, he had to believe that.

Didn't mean he didn't want to know what the apartment might look like.

The sound of hammering started up, the noise piercing his fucking skull. Right. No sleep for this guy. Time to go browbeat someone into letting him into the old man's apartment. After his shower.

He stumbled to the fancy-assed bathroom and got the water turned on, getting a bunch of spurts and hisses before the spray stabilized. The water looked clean and smelled normal, so Cullen scrubbed up, washing his hair and body with the same bottle of gel stuff.

The hot water lasted, which he'd worried about. As cold as Aspen was even in October and as old as this place was, it was a crap shoot. The only five-star amenity lacking in the bathroom was a towel warmer. He'd put in a request.

> *Dear Mr. Manager,*
> *Get me a fucking towel warmer.*
> *No love,*
> *Your boss.*

Okay, that was bitchy.

Still made him grin, didn't it? He dried off and found some sweats, just in case he decided to run.

The hammering hadn't let up a bit, the sound driving him out of the room. He had to find a quiet spot. Maybe in the basement, as he had last night.

He ran into someone who presented as a manager, and he latched on. "Hi. I'm Cullen. Did my granddad have an apartment?"

"I. Pardon me?" The guy was fifty, cue-ball bald with these eyebrows like wings that flew right up over his glasses.

"Cullen Patrick. Ben Patrick's grandson." He held out a hand to shake.

"Vic Mills. Pleased." He got a smile, which worked, even if the dude looked as if he wasn't sure what the fuck was going on.

"Nice to meet you. What do you do, Vic?" He headed the same direction the guy had been going, not wanting to delay him, really.

"I'm the service manager—housekeeping, maintenance, groundskeeping."

"Ah, the important parts."

The man's blue eyes twinkled. "All the parts are important, sir, but we are the heartbeat of the Treeline."

"How's the guts doing? I know plumbing is an issue."

"Slowly improving. Mr. Matt is committed to improving the infrastructure."

"Yeah? That's good, right? The bones have to be sound." Cullen chuckled. Listen to him, pretending he knew dick about hotels. Well, he'd stayed in a lot.

"Indeed. How can I help you?"

"Where did Grandpa stay?" He knew there had to be family stuff somewhere.

"His quarters are on the second floor, sir. You'll have to speak to Mr. Matt about access, I'm afraid. The master key doesn't open the private apartments. Only Mr. Matt can do that."

"Cool." Okay, the second floor. He could run some stairs again....

"Would you like me to page him, sir?"

"Nah. I don't want to bug him to death." In fact, Cullen was incredibly reluctant to be treated to that sad smile Matt had given him last night. He had a right to be here too, dammit.

He wasn't an asshole, at least not for the most part. Cullen just—he wanted to get to know Ben Patrick, even if it was too late.

"Well, I'd tell you to look for him in his office, but he's never there."

"No worries." He'd get the lay of the land first, then go after Matt. "Thanks for your help."

"Anytime." The walkie-talkie squawked, and Vic rolled his eyes. "Excuse me, please."

"Yep." He was on a mission now. Cullen was on the hunt for the private apartments.

He headed through the lobby, the place deserted and weird, echoing. Very Stephen King. *Come play with us, Cullen.* Man, he needed some sleep.

"Treeline, how can I help you?" Ah, he knew that voice. "No, sir, I'm sorry. I am completely booked for December and January. Yes, sir. I'm aware that you're a very important customer. Yes, sir. Let me check on that. Can you hold?"

Cullen trailed along, following Matt's noise until he found the man himself. Didn't they have a desk receptionist?

Matt was wandering down the hall, then began talking again. "I'm so sorry, sir. We're under renovation, and we simply don't have a room for those dates."

Cullen hated eavesdropping like a creep, but he didn't want to lose Matt before he got those keys.

"Yes, sir. I understand. Mmm-hmm. Disappointment is a powerful deterrent. Please accept our apologies. Good-bye." The button clicked off, and Cullen heard, "Entitlement whore. Fucking prick. I hope he gargles glass."

Ouch. Cullen had said worse, but it sounded as if Matt was having a shit day, and it was barely past brekkie. Oh. His belly rumbled, giving him away.

Matt spun around, offering him a look at a face that was as tired as his was in the mirror, before that perfect Hotel Manager mask fell.

"I find that wishing them a hot lava smoothie works too," Cullen said, the words popping right out.

Oh, that was a grin. A wicked grin. "I like it. I may have to borrow it."

Suddenly Matt seemed to be real, a real fucking dude. "I got it from a guy in Hawaii when I went surfing there." Cullen was suddenly reluctant to dim that smile with any requests. It was a good look for Matt.

"Yeah? It's a good one. I've never been to Hawaii. I'm not sure I remember sea level."

"You're not from here?" Matt didn't sound Colorado, but Cullen couldn't really place him.

"Houston, originally."

Texas. Wow. He didn't meet a lot of those on the circuit. *Not much on snow*, he thought.

"Neat. Why Colorado?" Cullen genuinely wanted to know.

"Ben hired me out of college to manage this place. I've never left."

"Wow. You've been here a bit, then. I mean, not that you're old."

"Yeah, on both accounts." Matt winked and then sighed. "Hold on. Treeline Estates, this is Matt, can I help you? Carrie, hey. Yeah. Yeah, we want to do the promotion. Do you need me to provide artwork or are you…? Oh, yeah? Good deal. No. No, that works. We'll be ready. Hmm? Sure. Sure, we're good."

Cullen waited, watching Matt deal with someone he appreciated, clearly. Advertising, he supposed.

"All right, honey. You take care, and e-mail me that file. I appreciate you."

There was the Texan right there. Wow. That was kind of fascinating.

Once Matt hung up, Cullen grinned at him. "Two things and I'll get out of your hair."

"Sure. What do you need?"

"Cereal." He laughed at Matt's surprised expression. "I don't want to bother anyone, but I didn't sleep, and I'm starving. And at some point, I want to make an appointment with you to see Grandpa's apartment." There. Abracadabra, diplomacy.

"Ah. One of those is easier than the other. Cereal is a breeze, but…." Matt blushed a dark red. "I have to admit I haven't been able to go back into the apartment since he left us. It's been professionally cleaned, but… I don't know. I just—It's like he's still here if I don't open the door." Matt's eyes went wide. "Cereal. Right. Come on."

"Cool." He got what Matt was saying, though. "My dad's place looks like one of those nuclear testing museums. I haven't touched it, really."

"Yeah? He wasn't my kin, but he was… my friend."

"He was family to you. You said that before. You don't have to feel weird about it. I mean, I feel assholish because I didn't know him, and that wasn't really my choice, you know?" Cullen shrugged. Family was a weird thing.

"He missed your dad, talked about him all the time."

"He did? Dad always said the old man would be glad he was gone." Wow. That sucked for—well, everyone. "Did he know anything about me?"

"No. Not even a clue. Ben would have been over the moon. He loved extreme sports."

"Really?" Okay, now there was an angle he could use later with the winter park thing. Much later. "Do you think I could look at the apartment on my own, then? I promise not to move anything or whatever. I just—I need to get to know him a little."

Matt shook his head, nodded, shook his head again. "Find me after you eat, and I'll open the room up for you."

"Thanks." Cullen grinned. "Cereal."

"Kitchen. I'll lead the way and grab a bagel."

"Awesome. I found the kitchen last night, but I'm not a hundred percent sure I could again." Wow. Things seemed better today. Hope sprang up in Cullen that he and Matt might get along.

"You can always call down, you know. Devlin is working standard hours."

"Oh, I hate to bother someone for a bowl of cereal." He'd call his new driver today and hit the grocery store.

They headed to the kitchen, a huge black man taking up the entire space by the stove. "Dev? Chef? This is Mr. Patrick, the owner."

"Well, hey! Ben's grandson, yeah? What a weird thing." Dev held out a hand for him to shake.

"Yeah, totally." And sort of sad, he guessed.

"Well, it's good to meet you. Bagel, Matt?"

"Please, sir. I'll take it with. I have to get with Nev."

"Sure, thing. Mr. Patrick?"

"Um. Cereal?" He hated to ask a chef for something so silly.

"We have Rice Krispies, Corn Chex, Frosted Mini-Wheats, and something chocolate."

"Oh, Chex would rock. Do you have almond milk?"

"Yes, sir. We have hemp, almond, and rice."

"Almond, then." He nodded happily. "Thanks so much!"

The bagel was popped in this rotating toaster deal before the cereal, milk, and bowl were handed over. He nodded before grabbing a stool off to one side. Bam. He loved Chex.

Matt took the bagel and headed out with a wave, on the phone again. How many times did the man have to say "Treeline Estates" a day?

"Why does he do reservations?" Cullen asked Dev, knowing he was prying but unable to let it go.

"Belinda's on maternity leave until November 15."

"Oh! Well, that makes sense." Man, he was just stumbling around in the dark and blundering into things. "Thanks for the omelet last night, by the way."

"You're more than welcome. It's boring, not having guests to cook for."

"Yeah? Do you do a staff meal at all?" That would be neat to sit in on if it didn't make everyone wicked uncomfortable.

"Twice a day. There's a continental breakfast in the staff lounge in the morning."

"Oh, rock on. I just hate to bother you." Cullen munched through his cereal.

"No bother. It's your food, after all."

"Yeah. I guess so." He laughed a little. You couldn't feed a trust, right? He would have to be the face of the owner.

"Well, there are croissant and biscuits, doughnuts, toast. Bagels for Matt."

"Croissant?" He'd had carrot cake. Cereal. He was carb loading as if he was about to compete.

"Yep. Want one?"

"Please?" He'd add another mile to his run. Seriously.

"You got it."

Like magic, pastry appeared. So did butter and jam, as well as a little plate of breakfast meats and some wee Danishes. Oh, God.

He was going to blow up and be a balloon.

Cullen moaned when he bit into the flaky thing, the buttery flavor bursting over him, the tart sweet of raspberry jam making his tongue curl against the roof of his mouth. It was totally worth it.

Totally.

He washed the whole thing down with some almond milk, then attacked the Danish. "Your pastry chef is amazing."

"I am. Thanks." He got a wink from Dev.

"Wow, you do sweet and savory. Did you cook for my grandpa?"

"Oh, for a while I did. The last few years, he wanted oatmeal and peanut butter."

"I can see that. Easy to eat, easy to digest."

"Yes, and he was tired of new things. Mr. Matt fed him, mostly."

"He was the old guy's best friend, huh?" It just seemed so odd to him. Nothing he'd been told about this place matched up.

"Yes, sir. Mr. Matt, well, he's a special kind of patient, isn't he?"

"I guess so." Cullen chuckled. "He didn't seem pleased to see me, but I have to admit, he's a decent guy."

"He's good. Are you going to keep him on, now that you're here to run the joint?"

Him? Run a hotel? He didn't think he could do that. "I sure hope Matt will stay. I have some investment ideas and all, but I'm no hotelier. Even when I retire from the circuit, I know I won't have the aptitude."

"I hope so too. Mr. Matt's a good manager and a fair boss."

"Everyone says that. It's great to hear." Cullen groaned and patted his belly. "He clearly hires good people."

"He does. The bad ones don't last. At all."

"By the way? Carrot cake. Two words. Ah-mazing."

"Good deal. I'm making German chocolate tonight."

"Add another mile." He made a checkmark in the air. "Thanks for letting me invade the kitchen."

"Lunch is at noon thirty. Turkey burgers and potato salad."

"I'll be here!" Noon thirty. He might could get in a run and a nap by then. He headed out, ready to hit the trail.

The view stole his breath. God, was there anything better than the mountains? Anything? Not to him. Cold air and snow, huge blue skies, and pine trees.

He found the trail easily, got going at a warm-up pace. By the time he got to running, he felt like a new man, as if he had this.

Now Cullen just had to figure out what to say to Matt Nathanson to make him stay.

## *Chapter Four*

**MATT** decided about three rooms in that painting was not for him. The guys needed help, and he was capable, if not willing. It was hot, tough work. Thank God he was only having to do the main parts of the walls. The detail work was for professionals.

Dip the roller, roll off the excess paint, paint in a *W* pattern....

He had his earphones on, since it was the middle of the night and he didn't have to answer the phones. He let the music fill his head, let the world disappear. Dip. Roll. *W*. Dip. Roll. *W*.

Adam Levine sang about animals and sugar, and Matt shook it a little, the paint fumes getting him light-headed. He stripped off his shirt, wiped the sweat away, and then discarded it. The guys should be pleased when they came in at eight. This would make their day so much easier.

Matt turned to pour more paint into his tray, and he caught sight of someone standing in the doorway, watching him. He blinked up, and for the weirdest second it was as if Ben had come back, a younger Ben, but Ben nonetheless.

Then Cullen smiled and kinda waved at him, and he shook off the feeling. Ben's grandson. Right. Not a ghost. "H… hey." He tugged out his earphones. "Was I making too much noise?"

"Nah. I couldn't sleep." Cullen held up his other hand, which held a tennis ball. "I play wall ball, and I'm taking advantage of no guests. You want some help?"

How was he supposed to answer that? He hadn't even seen Cullen since, was it two mornings ago?

Cullen's face fell. "Sorry. Sorry, you probably have a rhythm going."

"Maroon 5."

Cullen snorted out a laugh. "No, I mean working alone. There's German chocolate cake in the kitchen."

"Yeah?" Suddenly he was starving. Not hungry. *Starving.*

"Totally. I can help you finish up and clean up, if you'll come down and have some with me."

"Yeah. That would be…. Yeah. If you don't mind."

"Nope." Cullen came into the room and dropped his ball on the floor. "You need me to do brush work? I'll leave the close stuff for the crew, right?"

"Yeah. I'm just trying to get the crew a leg up. Give them a leg up?"

"Dude, I don't know." Cullen grabbed a paintbrush and got started. "I like the color."

"You and me both. The biddies at the historical society are going to hate it." It was a warm gray, not too dark, not too light. It was perfect.

"Really? I mean, gray was, like, big back in the day. Or at least that's what they tell me at the Stanley and Boulderado."

"They think I should use wallpaper."

"Wallpaper sucks in hotels," Cullen said, nose wrinkling.

"Yes. Yes, exactly." It got stained. It peeled. It bubbled and buckled.

"Yeah. Cabbage roses are so two centuries ago too."

The fact that Cullen knew a cabbage rose from a violet was impressive as hell. Matt had to smile. "Yep. I get what they're saying, but I kept the wainscoting."

"Good for you. Let's knock this out." Cullen grabbed a can and set to it, both of them painting away. The guy was pretty good, working hard, really putting paint on the wall. They managed pretty well, painting side by side, and he didn't even miss the music.

In fact, Matt blinked at the roller in his hand when they finished up about half an hour before he'd thought he would even be close to done. Nice.

"That's the last room for tonight." Matt offered Cullen his best smile and mostly sort of meant it. "I appreciate the help."

"No problem. I think I've earned cake." Cullen chuckled. "Where do we wash up? I know paint is bad for the bathrooms."

"There's a metal tub they left for me to wash the supplies."

"Oh, cool."

They cleaned up; then Matt led the way to the kitchen, which seemed to be a sort of neutral ground

for them. Cullen knew where the cake hid this time, and
Matt grabbed plates while Cullen cut slices.

Matt made himself a cup of coffee. "You want
one?" Not everyone was an addict like he was.

"Yeah, might as well. As long as there's cream."
Cullen winked. "Kind of an addict."

"To cream?" Was that a thing?

"Milk." Cullen plopped down on a stool. "Dad said
I was allergic."

"Oh, man. And you're not now?" He poured a
second cup.

"It can still make me all stuffed up, but that's pretty
much it." They traded coffee for cake. Not a bad deal.

He perched on a chair and dug into the sweet, his
belly telling him that he'd missed supper.

Cullen echoed his thoughts. "You didn't come to
supper. I think everyone blamed me."

"I must have worked through." He was spending
a lot of time in his own head right now, weighing his
options and sending out résumés.

"You want a sandwich? Pretty sure Dev left you a
Dagwood."

"Maybe when I'm done with my cake."

"Cool. Dev is an amazing baker. What a find he
was, I bet."

He had been. Dev was a rarity in the world—a
peaceful, happy chef who loved his job. Matt was
actually, basically, lucky, so far as his staff went. He
hoped they stayed that way once a new manager rolled
in, that the new guy would see what gems he had.

He thought whoever came on would. How could
they not? Management types loved this kind of
opportunity.

"Hey, you with me?" Cullen asked. "You're thinking way too hard."

"Am I? Sorry, I was just woolgathering. Are you settling in well?" He had to wonder whether Cullen would take Ben's apartment as his own.

"I still haven't gone to the apartment." Cullen shrugged. "I know I need to get out of your Presidential suite or whatever, but I feel weird."

"No one's using it." He had it booked for Christmas Eve, but that was it.

"That's good. Guess I'm more used to hotel rooms than not. Crazy, huh?" Cullen popped a piece of cake into his mouth. "Uhn."

"Yeah. It's good, and I wouldn't know from crazy. I've lived here since the dorms."

"No kidding. I mean, you said you came here out of college, but I didn't think you meant just." Cullen licked his fork. "So are you planning to leave?"

He let himself finish his bite while he decided on what to answer. Did he love it here? Yes. Did he hate Cullen? No. Did he think he could work for the rest of his life as a glorified manager because the real owner couldn't get rid of him? He wasn't so sure of that.

"I've been putting out some feelers, but if I resign, I'll give you thirty days' notice." That would be more than fair.

"Yeah? That's good. The staff love you, and I can see how much you're willing to work. I think we could come up with an agreement."

Somehow he wondered if it could be that easy. Matt very much doubted it.

"They're good people." And he knew it was stupid—to throw away a guaranteed job—but this wasn't a job. It hadn't been. This was going to be his life. This would have been his life? Was going to have been? Christ. Whatever. He'd gotten his hopes up and now he was butt-hurt.

"They are." Cullen tapped on the table, his body never completely still. "I need to get some practice in. Getting slow and lazy."

"Did you need a vehicle?" He wasn't sure how he was supposed to answer that.

"I have a driver." Cullen laughed, the sound a little wild around the edges. "I'm freaked out, and I have no idea what to do. I haven't even told my sponsors about this whole deal. What if they cut me loose?"

"Why would they?" That didn't make any sense "Ben was a good man, the business is legit, and everything is aboveboard."

"Well, because I have my own money now." Cullen chuckled. "Though I guess they know how much they paid me, right?"

"Yeah. They're paying for what your name can give them. That's all." It was simple as that.

"I feel like a bit of an idiot. I mean, I'm perfectly capable in my regular life, but I have no idea what to do about this." Cullen cut another piece of cake.

"No? I bet you'll figure it out. You're a smart guy." In another world, he would adore Cullen, and he thought they'd be fast friends.

"Yeah? I don't think I want to run a historic hotel, Matt." Cullen pinned him with a bright blue gaze, direct as hell. "I do have some ideas, but the hotel would be your baby."

"I'm not sure I can do it, Cullen. I don't know what I'm going to do. This is difficult."

"I bet. I've thought about it a lot, I guess. I really wanted to dislike you." That grin told Matt that Cullen wasn't managing that too well.

"I'm basically likable. Stodgy and a bit boring, but likable."

"You could use a makeover." Cullen hooted, the sound very owlish.

"Yeah, yeah. My average guest age is sixty-seven." He had to grin, though. Had to.

"Oh, shit, really? No wonder you don't have a gym!" Cullen stared, fork halfway to his mouth. "Dude, the clientele is gonna die out."

"There will always be sixtysomethings looking for a hotel, Cullen."

"Oh, right. Well, you are going to update the elevators?"

"I'm still trying to balance the look and the functionality."

"Yeah, if those two oldies but goodies go out, you're screwed."

"You're telling me. The elevators were both out from Valentine's to the Fourth the year Ben died."

"Oh, ew." Cullen shuddered. "I mean, I run stairs, but my dad would have left, you know? Boom. Deal breaker."

"It was a nightmare. Completely. We were all exhausted." Of course, he'd gotten a little ripped too, so that was cool.

"Tell me to stop shoving cake in my mouth." Cullen all but licked the plate.

"Do you have to starve yourself for the job?" He couldn't believe he asked, but he wanted to know.

"I have to watch my weight. I'm super lucky that if I increase activity, I can eat what I want. My trainer wants me to avoid white carbs." Cullen lifted his shirt, showing off a freaking eight-pack. "I do okay."

"Chocolate cake is totally not a white carb. Totally." His body gave a totally irresponsible response to the skin on display.

"No? Oh, rock on. It's dark carbs, right? German chocolate has coconut. All that good fat."

"Pecans." He could help with Cullen's carb loading "Again with the good fat."

"See? I knew you had my back. This is why I helped paint."

Yeah, he would imagine Cullen could eat anything, no back having needed. That body was stunning.

"I appreciate the help too. Seriously, man. I was worn out."

"You work crazy hours. You need an assistant."

"Oh, Belinda will be back soon, and life will ease up." He believed in maternity leave, dammit. Belinda worked her ass off; she'd earned the time.

"No, dude. I mean an assistant manager. Someone who can run here and there while you work on the big picture." Cullen was so cute. Naive. But cute. He not only didn't know how to find that elusive miracle employee, he wasn't even sure he was sticking around. "We'll see if it's in the budget," Cullen said, nodding sagely.

"See? I told you you'd get the hang of it."

"Lord. The budget thing is way easier when all you can afford is ramen. Trust me."

"Oh, believe me. I understand." There'd been a month where Ben hadn't let him buy supplies, and he'd been on a cracker diet for weeks.

"You want that sandwich?" Cullen stood, hovering by the small fridge Dev used to stash food for the crew.

"Yeah, I guess I will." He stretched up, his back cracking.

"Here, man." Cullen pulled out the sandwich before grabbing chips and pickles.

"You want to share?"

"Oh, hell. Sure, if you're good with it. I ran and ran today."

"Cool. We'll split it. This thing is insane." Huge and high and gorgeous. Dev was good to him. Matt grabbed the big bread knife and cut the sandwich in half while Cullen took out a plate.

The thing sort of held together. Mostly. Well, the pickles went sliding out.

Cullen rummaged in the fridge and came out with mustard. "Yum."

"Yeah. Watch for escapee pickles."

"Oh, I was gonna add more. If they're flying around that much. I'll work with what we got." Cullen looked five years younger at least.

"Eat the extras on the side, huh?"

"Good idea." Cullen laid out pickles and potato chips, counting them out.

That had to suck. He couldn't imagine. The pressure to stay in a certain weight range was something you equated with, like, boxers or jockeys, not snowboarders. "Do you enjoy it? Your job, I mean?"

"I do. I'm getting long in the tooth, but I love mountains."

"You're what? Six and a half? Maybe twelve?" He couldn't help the tease. He'd looked Cullen Patrick up, and he knew all the vitals. He believed in knowing your enemies, even when they ended up being less evil than an unfortunate accident of events.

"Yeah, that's me. Child prodigy." Cullen winked, then sobered. "I am thinking of coaching or something."

"Yeah?" That was a thing? "Do you have a coach?"

"Yeah. He's been with me long enough to let me coast on my own." Cullen chuckled. "I mean, I've got a trainer during the teeth of the season, and I have national team coaches on occasion. But it's getting to be a whole new world."

"Huh." That made… okay, it didn't make a lot of sense because Matt was the least athletic, graceful man alive, but he thought he got the gist. He'd thought coaches were supposed to be all day, every day people.

"Yeah." Cullen gave him a sideways, knowing look. "What else am I good at? I have to be able to con someone into giving me a job, and I'm too dude-like to be an announcer."

"Well, you do own a hotel, and I know that Ben left a number of investments, so that should be comforting." Dude-like. You'd think that would be a benefit for snowboarding announcing.

"I have an investment manager now. Can you believe it?" Cullen popped a pickle into his mouth.

Matt nodded and smiled. He'd worked with Dirk for quite a while, in Ben's stead. "You'll like him. He's a go-getter."

"Cool. I have some accounts he can work with." Cullen cut off a piece of sandwich, then pushed the rest toward Matt. "My eyes were bigger than my tummy."

He nodded, but he knew he'd wrap it up and save it for a quick snack tomorrow. Today. Whatever. He checked his watch. Three in the morning. Christ. "I have a meeting with the contractor at seven, so I'm going to excuse myself and go take a shower and a nap." Matt stood up and wrapped his plate up and stowed it away.

"Sure." Cullen rose and grabbed the plate to take with him. "Night. Thanks for letting me butt in."

"Thank you for the help." Matt made sure everything was closed up and made the trip up the stairs to his quarters, exhaustion riding him hard.

His brain wasn't any closer to making any decisions, either.

Maybe he just needed to let it ride. Just one more day.

## Chapter Five

**THE** place seemed to be humming with activity when Cullen crawled out of his room about ten o'clock. He knew he'd missed breakfast, so he wasn't sure what was happening, but staff members were… scurrying? Was that the word?

He grabbed one of the little maids. "Hey. Everything okay?"

"Mrs. Allen and Mrs. Kirkwilde are here, and Mr. Matt is… well, it's not my place. Would you like me to order you breakfast?"

"Who are Mrs. Allen and Mrs. Kirkwilde?"

She looked at him with huge, dark eyes and whispered. "The historical society ladies."

"Oh." Oh, man. He could just imagine how these ladies must look.

She nodded. "I'm going to stay up here and out of sight."

"I'll protect you." He wasn't dressed for meeting with the old ladies' aid society, but in jeans and a long-sleeved T he looked better than usual. Might as well jump into the fray.

"You should hide. They're enough to make Mr. Matt snarl."

"I'm not scared." He winked, then patted her on the shoulder on the way by.

"We didn't approve that color, Matt. Change it," one of the old ladies was saying.

"It's not going to happen, Mrs. Allen. The color is clean, easy to care for, and already on the walls." Matt's voice was slightly chilly, heading into cold.

"But it's not on the approved list—"

"The suggested list. Guest rooms are not subject to your rubber stamp. I'm using period colors and furnishings, but making the modern guest comfortable, as well."

*Listen to that. Impressive.* Cullen hadn't been able to meet that part of Matt yet.

The other lady spoke up. "Matthew, your clientele is far more comfortable with our choices."

"This is the color the rooms are going to remain, Mrs. Kirkwilde."

"Matthew, it seems you're getting a little big for your britches. Perhaps we should simply speak to the new owner."

"Pardon me?" Oh. Oh, that was frosty.

Cullen trotted down the steps, turning on his "I'm new here" smile. "Morning, Matt. What's up?"

"Good morning. Mrs. Kirkwilde, Mrs. Allen, this is Ben's grandson, Cullen." Matt's expression resembled a granite rock face with no handholds.

"Really?" The Kirkwilde lady wiggled in a way older ladies only did in movies. Weird. "So good to meet you."

"Thanks." He shook hands gingerly. "I dig the paint."

"Well, Cullen, the problem is that your general manager didn't get approval first."

"He just said he didn't need it for the guest rooms." Cullen gave her a sunny smile. "Now if Matt's anything, he's meticulous. He's done his research."

Matt was going to explode. Cullen could feel the threat in the air, which was pretty cool, given that they didn't really know each other yet. It would almost be worth letting it happen too, just to see it.

Then again, Matt might unload on him, which would suck.

"He really needs to work with us if he wants to maintain a good relationship," the other lady said with a sniff.

"I have been working with you. However, I do not work for you, nor do I work for Mr. Patrick here. I work for the Treeline Estates, and my job is to run the property in the way I deem best. At this point, I believe the colors in the guest rooms are fully appropriate. They echo the colors used in the lobby and the granite on the stairs. The colors are attractive, clean, and not currently under discussion." The madder Matt got, the more Texan he sounded.

Cullen wondered if it worked that way when Matt was turned on too.

Whoa. Where did that come from, and could it come at a more inappropriate time? Hello? Down, boy.

Cullen waited for the next hysterical society salvo, feeling as if he were watching a tennis match.

"Well, I never!"

Matt shook his head. "You have. We both have, and I've given in on some points, but this one is moot. The walls are painted, I'm legally in the right, and I have final say."

When the women both turned on Cullen, he held up both hands. "He's right. He has the power." If his voice slipped into a Schwarzenegger impersonation, well, so be it. He had a lot of Austrian friends.

Matt covered up a snort with a faked sneeze.

Nice. Cullen chuckled, drawing outraged glares. "Sorry, ladies, I can be inappropriate. Professional athlete. Hazard of the job."

"If you want, you can see the work happening around the main fireplace in the library. It's nearly complete. Otherwise, there's nothing new. Most of the work has been structural."

"The library, if you please."

"Sure. Henry?" Matt turned to a well-dressed young man who had appeared out of nowhere. "Take the ladies to the library? Feel free to call me if there are any concerns, but I'm afraid I'm on a tight schedule today."

Cullen waited until the ladies were out of earshot. "Wow. Dragons."

"Fire-breathing." Matt was all growls and grumpiness.

Cullen didn't blame him. "Sorry if I was out of line. I figured you could use some backup."

"You're the owner. I don't know that you even have an out of line."

"Yeah, and if you're leaving, I guess I need to get used to dealing with them." Wow, that was a depressing thought. Matt leaving.

"You're leaving?" Yvonne stood there, eyes wide. "You can't! Where would you go? What the hell are you thinking, leaving us?"

Dev groaned, hands full of a tray of pastries. "No! No leaving. This is a good job."

"Oh, for God's sake. Calm down. The ladies are still here." Matt's voice brooked no argument.

"Shit. Sorry." Cullen grabbed a pastry, hoping no one would whack him.

"You can't leave us. Things are just starting to turn around. To have hope." Dev offered Matt the side with a bagel. "You look tired, boss."

"I am. Everyone needs to get back to work. We'll have a staff meeting once the gorgons are gone." Matt took a bagel, offering Dev a half smile. "Seriously, let's get them out the door, huh?"

"Sure." Dev nodded easily but glanced at Cullen as if for reassurance.

So Cullen nodded and smiled. "It's all good, guys. I was just talking out my ass."

Because, goddammit, Matt loved this stupid fucking hotel and the amazing fucking people in it, and he wasn't leaving. Cullen had no idea how he would make Matt stay, but he would.

Starting now. "Can I walk with you?" Cullen grabbed one more pastry and began shooing everyone else off.

"Sure. Sure, what do you need, Cullen?"

"Well, first I want to apologize for butting in just now and getting everyone all ramped up." Cullen felt as though he needed to say that because he hadn't meant to cause panic.

"You don't have to apologize. You were telling the truth. I'm…." Matt stopped, took a deep breath, and shook himself as if he was shaking off a bad dream. "What did you really need, Cullen?"

"I need some coffee. I need you to take me to Ben's apartment so I can see what needs to be done there. I need you to tell me you'll stay on as the manager."

"I don't have time, Cullen."

"Make time. We have to do this. You. Me. Coffee. Ben's apartment."

If nothing else, Matt needed to roust this ghost. His grandfather had obviously loved Matt, and he didn't believe for a second that Matt hadn't taken care of Ben. Good care. So, the least he could do was help Matt move on. The man would never agree to do anything new and different with Grandpa's specter hanging over him.

Matt blinked at him. "I guess I have time to unlock the door."

"Good. Thank you. First, we both need coffee." Matt looked like shit walking. Maybe he'd get the man to lie down, take a goddamn nap.

"Oh, we can order coffee and have them bring it to us there." Matt started back up the stairs toward the second floor, tugging out his little phone.

"Dev, can you have someone bring us a coffee for two up to Ben's apartment, please?" Matt chuckled. "Yes, and more pastry and maybe some sausage or bacon or—Right."

Cullen grinned. He was going to be a round little dumpling by the time Matt was finished feeding him. He would have to get that gym put in, even if he just told Matt it was for the staff to begin with. A perk of working at the Treeline.

Somewhere full of windows so he could watch the snow falling as he worked out.

That sounded magical.

Cullen bounced along after Matt, tickled as shit now that he'd made a decision of sorts. The Treeline would be his home base from now on, and he'd see where he stood after this season as far as retiring from snowboarding.

Matt led him up to the door of Ben's apartment and unlocked the door with a steady hand and his lips pursed. "It needs a dusting and an airing out, but it's clean."

Cullen stepped past Matt, the smell of cleaner the most prevalent. He guessed he'd expected it to have old-man smell.

There was crap everywhere—not filth, but clutter. Books, magazines, knickknacks, framed photographs, weird-assed crystal decanters. It was like a junk store or something.

Cullen didn't say it because he had no intention of hurting Matt's feelings, but whoa. Fifty years of stuff all crammed into one place.

Matt stood at the doorway, looking in for a long minute before stepping inside the rooms.

"You okay?" Cullen asked, at a loss as to where to start.

"Yeah. Yeah, I am. He loved all this stuff. I think it comforted him or something. That's a fireplace, you know? That wall there, that's all paneling? He decided the monsters were going to crawl out, so we hid it, but it's lovely."

"Are you—attached to any of this? I mean, not the furniture and all, but the papers and knickknacks." Cullen would clear that out and start over. He enjoyed antiques better than most guys his age. He chuckled. So queer sometimes.

"I don't know. I suppose I should go through all of them and decide whether or not they're important."

"Sure. I mean, we can make a staging area and do that a little at a time." The idea of spending a lot of time that way with Matt appealed to him.

Matt shot him a curious little look, then went back to wandering, just looking around no doubt remembering. Cullen felt more as if he was learning Matt, not his grandpa. The things Matt touched, the one thing he picked up, these all had to be important to him for some reason.

"This is a picture of your grandmother and your dad. Ben told me he took it when they were hiking in Maroon Bells."

"Oh, wow." He loved Maroon Bells. The place was downright magical. He had no idea his dad had ever been there. "Look at that."

"Yeah. He loved her a lot. I think it damn near destroyed him when she passed."

"Dad never talks about her. Talked." Cullen traced the picture with one finger.

"He was little. Five or six?"

"Right. I'm sorry I missed his stories, though." Okay, no getting maudlin. He couldn't redo his childhood, and why should he? He'd had a decent kidhood or whatever.

"I bet. Ben told me lots." Matt looked around the apartment. "Is there something you're looking for specifically, or are you just curious?"

"I'm looking to see if I can move in, Matt. I can sell Dad's place in Park City."

Matt blinked at him, then blinked again. "Oh. Right." Matt nodded and ducked his chin, going to straighten some papers on the huge mahogany desk.

"Hey, I'm not wanting to manage the hotel. I mean, at all. I might make some suggestions."

A waiter knocked on the door, with the coffee. That was good. They could sit and have coffee and talk like people.

Matt took the coffee, offered the kid a five, and brought the tray to the desk. They both poured a cup, then sat, one at the desk, one on the couch.

"So, talk to me, dude," Cullen finally said. "You gonna hang out and fight the historical ladies for me?"

Matt stirred his coffee, eyes on his cup. "I don't have the collateral yet to buy my own place, so I suppose I'm going to stick around and restore the Treeline."

"Woo. I mean, not that you don't have the funds, but I think we can do well together."

"I hope so. So, you're moving in to these quarters?"

"I think so, yes. I mean, I guess I still need to look around, but they're big rooms, the furniture rocks, though if there's anything you want, or that's like, important to the hotel, it's yours."

"Let me show you where the other rooms are. There's a master, a second bedroom, and a bath."

"Oh, wow. That's rad."

Matt chuckled softly, then opened the door to the left of the desk. There was the bathroom and two bedrooms—one filled with boxes, one empty for the most part.

Cullen could totally see redoing the bathroom, but honestly it was way more blank slate than he'd expected.

"We had to send the hospital furniture back."

"He was on hospice?" His dad had done that. Lord what a mess.

"Yeah. The last few weeks were brutal, but he didn't want to leave here."

"You're a good guy, Matt. I know how tough that is." Cullen had taken three months off the tour when his dad was at the end.

"He was my best friend."

Cullen wasn't sure if that was dear or sad. He was gonna go with dear. Everyone needed a best friend, even crazy old dudes. "I'm sorry." Had he said that? "So, how about we do one stack of papers now, and then you can get back to real life?"

"Sure." Matt sat at the big desk, and he looked right at home, as if he'd been in the chair a thousand times.

Cullen pulled up another chair after he grabbed a box out of the other room. "Keep, toss, and decide piles?"

"You read the organizational magazines too, huh?"

"Lots of time in lobbies and airports." Cullen chuckled. "I draw the line at washi tape. Not manly."

"What the fuck is washing tape?" Matt blinked, then clapped his hand over his mouth.

"Washi. Japanese thing. My buddy Aaron? His girlfriend is totally into it. It's masking tape you decorate shit with." He knew lots of arcane crap.

"Ah. Good to know." Matt rolled his eyes. "Not my thing."

The first pile of papers was all financial and needed shredding. The second was a mixture of weird-assed notes about the hotel. "What does this note about the gazebo mean?" Cullen handed over a scrawled note with drawings.

"Oh, just something Ben and I had played around with. It's nothing."

"Where would it go?" It looked neat, as if they could do weddings in it and shit.

"I thought we could put it back where you can see the mountains, the pasture, but Ben didn't like the idea."

"Why not?" Cullen tilted his head. "Did he think it would spoil the view?"

"No changes, kid." Suddenly Matt's voice changed, the imitation oddly resembling Cullen's father's voice. "There's a reason this place is special. No. Changes."

"Ouch." Cullen nodded slowly. "But you don't feel that way, right? I mean, I know you want to keep the integrity of the hotel and all, but there's more you could do."

"I honestly don't know. I'm not in a place to know anything. A week ago this wasn't a job, and now it is, but you can't even fire me. I'm still working my shit out."

"Sure." Cullen reached out, not even thinking about it, and touched Matt's shoulder. Offering comfort, oddly enough. He sucked at this stuff, at the hard stuff. Usually he just ran. Matt's confusion was a palpable thing, something in the air. He wasn't responsible for it, but he sort of was, and he wanted to… hell, he didn't know. He wanted to ease Matt's mind.

Matt leaned into the touch for a moment, eyes closing. Yeah, this guy wasn't used to being anything but someone else's rock.

Cullen wasn't Mr. Comforting as a rule, but Matt needed…. Shit, Matt needed a fucking nap.

Cullen chuckled, patting Matt's shoulders in a half hug now. "You look so tired."

"Long day or two." Matt stretched up, giving him a glimpse of a flat belly, a surprisingly respectable six-pack under the man's T-shirt.

Cullen's mouth went dry, and he sat with that surprising feeling for a long moment. No, no analyzing. Matt was an attractive guy, and Cullen was a gay man. He didn't have to get all grumpy because a bare belly made him happy.

He wet his lips, shook his head. Huh.

"You okay?" Matt asked, easing back from him.

Shit, was he being stupidly obvious? Awkward. "I'm fine."

"Cool. Well, I'll…. Here." A single key on a ring was offered over. "This is Ben's key."

"Thanks." Cullen took it, knowing that had to be tough, that Matt was telling him something important.

"Good deal. Holler if you need me. I'm going to get back to work." Matt offered him a tired smile and grabbed his coffee cup on the way out the door.

"Get some rest at some point!" he called. Cullen would start with the empty bedroom, make a list of what he needed.

Then maybe he'd see if there was any new powder anywhere nearby.

He needed to get a motherfucking car too. Maybe he should call Brandon, get some suggestions. He'd keep the guy on retainer for the hotel, but he needed to be able to get around on his own.

His phone rang, and for a moment he forgot what the ringtone meant. Had it been that long since someone called? Then he clicked it open, answering the call from his sports agent, Paul. "Hey, man, what's up?"

"Cullen! How's it going? Did you get your family business taken care of? I'm sorry, again, about your grandpa."

"Yeah, thanks. Uh, it's complicated, but I'm getting there." That seemed the easiest way to put it.

"Cool. You think you can free up a few days? I got you a Mountain Dew commercial."

"Wow." He grimaced, glad Paul couldn't see him. He hated that sticky sweet stuff, but that was a great deal. "Sure. Just let me know."

"They want you in Aspen this week, if they can. They prefer to run the spot during the games."

Oh, hell yeah. He was, like, right here. A commercial that didn't require travel? Hoo yeah.

"I can totally do that, Paul. I'm maybe half an hour away, even with bad weather. Hell, I even have a place for the crew to stay if we have enough rooms renovated by the time you get here."

"Excellent. I'll send you the pertinent deets. You sound happy, Cul. I approve."

"Do I?" Cool. Maybe he was. "I've been in one place for a week."

"Whoa. And you didn't turn to stone?"

"No moss or anything," Cullen teased. "I know, right? I need to find a place to practice, but otherwise I'm like a pig in shit."

"Well, you ought to have mountains, and the snow is falling."

"Yep. I just need to figure out where I can get a run in. I trust you on the ad thing, you know that."

"I do. Give me a holler if you have questions, and I'll get that e-mail out to you."

"Rock on." E-mail was a fab thing. There would be contracts and all, but he'd sign electronically.

He clicked off and looked around the room. It was a good space, or it would be. He wanted to…. Oh. The fireplace was still all blocked up. Cullen wanted to get into that bitch and see. He called down to the front desk and got Matt.

"Treeline Estates, how can I assist you?"

"You can get an assistant. Dude, how do you get anything done?" Cullen teased.

"I'm Superman. Belinda will be back to work soon. What do you need?"

"Maintenance. Who's your maintenance dude, again?"

"Vic. Vic Mills. Bald guy, huge eyebrows?"

"Right! Can you get me to him?" Cullen asked.

Matt chuckled. "I'll share his contact with you. I have him in my phone."

"You rock. Nap soon. Seriously."

"Yeah, yeah." Matt snorted. "I might fall over. Same idea, you know?"

"So not. Thanks." Cullen wanted a sledgehammer. Woo! Demo!

Soon he had a sledgehammer, a crowbar, a bunch of screwdrivers, and the admonition not to hurt himself, release a demon, or let any rabid bats into the hotel.

Vic managed all this sangfroid.

His dad had made him work construction one summer to replace a snowboard he'd broken with some careless rail sliding. So he knew the basics. "Got it. No otherworldly bat monsters," Cullen said, solemn as a preacher.

"Good deal. Of course, if one shows up, video first, call me second. We'll have a blast."

Cullen liked Vic. A lot. "You got it." He saluted smartly.

Vic snorted and headed back to work.

Okay. He needed to make a few exploratory taps with a hammer first. No messing up a mantle or anything.

Matt had been right. The paneling was just cursorily stuck up there, just tapped in, and he had it down in minutes. The fireplace was old and huge, with enough room in the hearth to roast an elephant or at least a turkey.

The mantel had these amazing carvings, though the wood had been painted white, then gray with maybe a bright green in there. Cullen wanted to strip it down and stain it. "I wonder if there are hardwoods under this carpet?"

Before he knew it, he was half-naked, throwing windows open, and in desperate need of a Dumpster. He called Vic again. "Hey, no demons, but uh, how do I get rid of all this detritus?"

"I'll send a couple of the day laborers up."

"I made a mess. I'm happy to clean up, I just need to know what and where." This was hard work. Great cardio.

"There are a metric ton of construction Dumpsters in the back. Just head down the freight elevator. The doors are propped open."

"Oh, cool. I'll holler again if I need guys." This was kinda fun. Cullen could see why people flipped houses.

"Yes, sir."

At some point, someone knocked and delivered him a platter of sandwiches and potato chips. Cullen tipped the kid before whipping out his phone to text Matt.

*Thanks for lunch! There's cookies. Come eat.*

Matt was like…. Hotel Claus. Santa Hotel? That was weird. Also, the very idea of Matt in a Santa suit was so disturbing that Cullen shoved that image into a time-out. Boom.

*YW. Save me one?*

*U got it.*

He had enough to save one of everything.

The wood beneath the carpet was stunning, and he could already see the rooms glowing.

Cullen bounced. Then he washed up so he could munch a pickle and a turkey BLT. Uhn.

He was done eating when Matt knocked, and Matt's eyes went wide when Cullen opened the door. "Wow."

"I should have warned you. I got trigger happy, huh? Come on and eat. There's a sandwich in the fridge. Coke or tea?"

"Coke, please. You've been busy. Do you need someone to help?" Matt looked as if he was going to pass out with exhaustion.

"Nope. Vic told me where the Dumpsters were. When the carpet goes, I'll get someone." He could probably dump it out the window, but he'd get the all clear first. "The carpet in the guest room still looks really good."

"That's been storage for years."

"So what all is in the boxes?" Cullen got Matt set up with food and a Coke and began munching a cookie.

"Crap. I mean, there's just tons of stuff Ben couldn't part with."

"Oh." Maybe he should have a charity sale for the hotel? Cullen added that idea to his growing mental list. He'd write it all down tonight.

"I'll have it moved to the basement, if you want."

"Oh, I'm not in any hurry. No one I know would rather stay with me than in a room at the hotel." That was probably telling Matt too much about his life, or lack thereof.

Matt nodded, ate another cookie, and stared at the fireplace. "I love that crazy beast of a thing."

"It's amazing. Do you know what kind of wood is under there? I want to take it back down and stain it." He watched a lot of *Rehab Addict* marathons in hotel rooms.

"Everything else is mahogany, so that would be my guess."

"Cool. I'll get Vic to get me some stripper and sandpaper."

"In the basement. We have a ton of stuff down there."

"Ghosts?" he teased.

"Zombies are infinitely more likely."

"Slow zombies are okay. Fast ones, no." Cullen ate another cookie. Dev was worth his weight in gold, those things were so good.

"Nothing here is fast. This place is slow."

"That's okay." Maybe slow was what Cullen needed. "What's your favorite thing about the hotel?" he asked.

"Do you mean the actual building?"

"In general. You can break it into categories, I guess." More chips. They needed more chips. "Do you think Dev would make us more kettle chips?"

"You're the boss." Matt grabbed his phone, dialed. "Dev, Mr. Patrick needs more chips."

Cullen blinked, deflating a little. Right. He was the boss. Matt wasn't hanging out because he wanted to or anything. Cullen had forgotten for a moment they weren't just friends.

Matt laughed softly, then met his eyes. "Dev says Cullen can have more—Mr. Patrick can kiss his ass."

He cracked up. "Well, Cullen was the one who asked. I swear."

"Okay, so Cullen needs chips, please, sir. Enough for two."

Trying not to beam was hard, but he was tickled Matt was staying. Chuffed, as his one Australian buddy would say.

"I hope that's okay if I snatch a few?" Matt's hand hovered over the plate.

"Hell, yeah. I was hoping you'd come feed with me." Now he felt better. Lighter. Like a dork.

"Feed with you?" Matt chuckled softly.

"Yep. Strap on ye olde feedbag. Nosh. Nom. Graze. I'm going to update your stodgy slang."

"Stodgy?" One eyebrow climbed up Matt's forehead.

"You said it. Or something akin to it. Before." *Nice, Cullen.*

"Yeah. Well, I'm a hotel manager whose best friend was eighty-six. I'm old."

"But see, you're not. Dude, come snowboarding with me tomorrow. I'll give you a lesson."

"Snowboarding? Me?"

Jesus, like Matt was a hundred years old or something. He couldn't be much older than Cullen, if at all. "Totally. That way you can see what kind of winter fun there is to be had around here. I mean, how old can you be?"

Matt pinked, but Cullen thought the man's grin looked pleased.

"I've got some gear you can borrow." Or they could hit a ski shop. Cullen got a great discount on certain brands thanks to his sponsors.

"Maybe. I'm not much older than you, I bet. I've got work to do, but…. Yeah. Maybe."

"Nope. Pencil me in. Lunchtime snowboard lesson. Just think how many people you can recommend the ski area to once you've seen it."

The chips came, and they fell on them, talking about movies and television, weird music. Matt enjoyed some really good stuff, especially in movies, and Cullen confessed his super unpopular love of classic country music.

Matt was fading, dozing off, and Cullen knew the man needed rest. He got Matt moved to the old sofa that he'd pushed out of the way to move the carpet.

"I can't."

"Sure you can. No worries." He palmed Matt's phone and turned it to silent. He'd answer it if anyone called.

He covered Matt up with a blanket, the man's eyes already closed. The deep, even breathing told him in no time Matt had dropped off, so Cullen turned his phone on vibrate too, before heading to the guest room to go through one box. One at a time, right?

He grinned at the sight of Matt, sound asleep as if he hadn't rested in weeks. That was what he liked to see. Peace.

Everyone deserved to sleep. Rest made all things easier.

Even dealing with a new hotel owner, he guessed.

## Chapter Six

**MATT** checked the newly renovated rooms and nodded. Yeah. Things were starting to look reasonable. He jogged downstairs to grab his bagel and coffee and see how plans for the sneak-peek cocktail party were going.

The kitchens were bustling, Dev having brought in two extra sous chefs and a baker, plus the waiters. "Hey, Matt! How's it hanging?"

"Busy-busy, as always." Matt popped his bagel in the toaster. "Things getting shaped up for tomorrow night?"

"Lord, yes." A wide, white smile split Dev's face. "Did a trial run on the macarons today. They're amazing."

"Ooh. Can I try one?"

"Yep. Hazelnut or passion fruit?"

"Hazelnut." He didn't get the whole passion fruit thing. Weird, slimy eyeball things, but the European crowd dug it.

Dev reached into a cabinet and whipped out a wee plate with three cookies arranged on it. They were uniform in size, a toasted coffee color, and they smelled like heaven in a nut. "Oh, you are a master. Save some back for Cullen. He's doing that commercial."

"Right. I'm making you two spaghetti and meatballs for supper. Salad. Garlic bread."

Somehow, Matt and Cullen had started eating supper together most nights. "Thank you. You're good to us."

"I try. That way I can have an easy staff meal tonight. Does that work?" Dev looked uncertain all of a sudden. "Cullen said if it wasn't in the budget, he'd cover it."

"We can pay the bills, Dev. Don't worry." He was in charge of the budget, and he would worry about it, dammit. Ben had left enough in the trust to do everything Matt wanted to do if he didn't make a profit for two years. That and he knew Cullen was trying to help.

Still, they would turn a profit next year. He had no doubt. Right?

"Cool. I just didn't want to overstep. These guys have been polishing silver and wiping down glasses and cooking their asses off."

"Good deal. Everyone from the historical society will be here, along with the mayor and some locals." He was dreading it. The schmoozing made his head feel as though it might explode. There was a movie from years ago where someone practicing their speech said, "Just give me the goddamn money."

That was how Matt felt about approval from the people constantly sticking their nose into his business.

"You're going to do fine, boss. You're magic." Dev grinned at him, but he knew better.

"Maybe I can con Cullen into pretending to be me." Cullen worked the whole snowboarder "dude" angle hard, but Matt had seen the man go over a contract for a commercial opportunity.

One way or the other, Cullen had the charm thing down. Matt chuckled.

Dev raised an eyebrow. "Did you really snowboard?"

"No. I made it up the lift, and Vic and Nev called about the leak in the boiler."

"I tried skiing once the year I moved here," Dev said. "That went poorly."

"Yeah. It's not for all of us." He sighed softly and stretched. "Okay. Back to work. Man, I need a vacation."

"You so do." Dev grabbed his arm. "Bagel."

"Uh-huh. Bagel. Coffee?"

"What do you want?" Dev was a whiz with the espresso machine.

"Hazelnut latte?"

"Extra whip?"

"Promise you won't tell?"

"Your froufy coffee secret is safe with me." Dev laughed, the big, booming sound making Matt smile.

"Thanks, buddy."

"Anytime."

Matt answered e-mails and ate his bagel, his mind going a million miles an hour. It was crazy how he sort of missed Cullen's easygoing presence. This was the first day he hadn't seen Cullen at all by ten o'clock, and yeah. Weird.

Still, how interesting was a commercial—a real commercial?

His phone chimed softly, and he glanced at it, chuckling when he saw a selfie of Cullen and a Dew bottle.

*Impressive*, Matt sent back.

Okay, that was cool. The next shot was even cooler, because someone had taken a picture of Cullen doing some aerial maneuver.

The sight made his mouth dry, more than a little, and it threatened to make other parts of his body unsightly. When had that happened? That Matt had started thinking of Cullen as yummy?

Cullen was, for all intents and purposes, his boss and totally off-limits. Not just the boss, but Ben's family. Boss, family and, come on. Matt was a boring guy. *Stodgy* was Cullen's word.

Of course, the way Cullen looked at him sometimes....

Stop it.

*You look great. Can't wait to see the commercial*

*Thx! Bored now*

He snorted. Cullen had told him there was a lot of sitting around and waiting at a shoot.

*I'm eating and having a latte. Envy me.*

*Bagel city.*

Cullen knew his eating habits well by now. Bagel and coffee. Grilled cheese for lunch. Big salad for supper. Unless he was eating with Cullen.

Cullen ate… everything. The man was fearless.

From carrots to cake or a mix of the two. Cullen enjoyed sushi, steaks, and sesame chicken. Dev already adored the man.

Matt sent another text.

*Hazelnut latte, though*

*Oooh brave. Go you! Testing new Dew flavors on the crowd here*

*Good man.*

Were they friends? Did he want to be friends with Cullen? He knew the man had all sorts of ideas for the land around the hotel. He'd been putting off the meeting Cullen kept asking for. He knew what Ben had wanted. Ben wanted this place to be caught in time.

Matt wasn't so sure that was the way to go, but he was stuck. He didn't want to alienate the clientele who preferred the historical hotel, but he couldn't see being stuck in the past.

He didn't want to terrify them either. It was a delicate thing.

Cullen was… a conundrum. Hot, sweet, both younger and far older than his age. Eager to help but occasionally overstepping. And Cullen made him feel… funny.

Deep inside. Like no one else ever had.

One of the bellmen ran up, panting hard. "Boss? The sink in the convention area men's room is going off like Old Faithful."

"Huh." He grabbed his latte and ran, texting the plumber on the way.

There was never really enough time to sit and think about shit. Not if he was doing his job. God knew that was what he was good at. He loved it too, and he was beginning to think he could still do this. So much that he'd turned down an assistant manager position in Durango.

Assistant manager. Fuck that.

"Never take a lateral or a demotion," Ben would tell him. "Claw your way up, not down."

Someone would have to offer him management of a chain. That would definitely be up.

He chuckled. Sure. Oh, he loved Treeline. Maybe he would make this work. One way or the other, he had to patch some leaks and get the job done.

**"WE** should go to dinner." Cullen had been helping Matt pick out carpet patterns. A mill in North Carolina had submitted three samples of an updated version of the Treeline's original carpets. They all had great points, but there was one that really said "antique hotel with a fresh new look."

"Pardon?" Matt looked up at him, dark eyes warm, happy.

"We did this momentous rug picking. We should go to Aspen."

"Momentous rug picking." Matt laughed softly, nodded, shook his head, nodded again.

"Yep. Hungry work. Tightrope walking with the historical society, making sure it feels good, under foot…. We deserve a reward."

"I guess there's no reason we can't. I haven't been out to supper in a while."

"Rock on! Do you have a favorite place?"

"I like the bar menu at L'Hostaria."

That seemed to surprise Cullen, that Mr. Accommodating had an opinion. Well, not had one, but shared it. "Italian, right? Sounds good. Split a couple of apps and then suck down some pasta?"

"Okay. Sure. Let's do it."

"Cool. You need to get out more." Cullen winked, and there was no malice in it.

"Yeah, yeah. Shut up."

"It's true. I'm tickled you're going with me." Cullen bounced.

Matt felt his cheeks heat, but he couldn't have fought his smile for love or money. Cullen was so... joyful. So young in spirit. Matt was barely over thirty, but sometimes he felt older than old Ben.

Cullen made him feel both ancient and younger somehow, all at once. Whatever it was, Matt was learning that he wanted to explore Cullen's world.

"Come on. Go put on something nonmanagerial."

"Like what?" Oh, man. Did he have....

"Dark jeans. Nice shirt. No tie."

"No tie?" He had jeans. They weren't pressed, though....

"Nope. None. Not even a bow tie."

Matt resisted the urge to stick his tongue out. Instead he shot Cullen a salute. "All right, then. I will do my best."

"Good deal. Meet me downstairs in an hour." Cullen winked at him and headed out, a spring in his step.

"Lord." He needed to press his shirt, his jeans. Not managerial. What the fuck did that mean? Matt shook his head. His head was spinning.

It didn't take him long to get dressed, answer all the phone calls coming in, and deal with a half-dozen e-mails. An hour flew by, and he was about five minutes late meeting Cullen down in the lobby.

Holy moly, Cullen cleaned up well. He wore a pair of dark green cargo pants, a cobalt button-down shirt, and a pair of real shoes. The shirt made Cullen's shoulders look amazing.

He caught himself staring, blinking a little.

Yummy.

Cullen caught sight of him, a grin breaking over that face, the high cheekbones and bright eyes dangerously attractive. "Check you out! You do own jeans. I knew they'd be Wranglers."

He shrugged. What could he say? He was from Texas.

Cullen looked him over slowly, his smile going all Cheshire cat. "It's a good look for you."

Oh. His cock filled in a rush, stealing all the blood from his brain. Hell, he almost stared down at his crotch in amazement, because he couldn't remember the last time that had happened anywhere but late at night when he was in bed.

Cullen didn't even pretend not to notice. No, in fact Cullen licked his lips and stared just below Matt's belt buckle.

That didn't help.

It didn't help at all.

"We should go." Right?

Cullen cleared his throat. "We totally should. I called and got us a table, just in case they got busy."

"Very nice. Someone might think you were organized and stuff."

"You must be rubbing off on me." Cullen blinked, then laughed, cheeks hot pink. "You know what I mean."

Matt couldn't have fought his grin even if he wanted to. He nodded slowly. "I do. Good thing too. A man might get the wrong idea." Was he flirting? He thought he was, which was ridiculous. He didn't

flirt, and he'd just gotten used to the idea of Cullen
as a friend, not a—something else. That wasn't going
to work.

Not ever.

But Cullen made him want to, didn't he? Matt grew
to admire the man more each day, from his willingness
to work, to his good-natured acceptance of their strange
working relationship. He thought maybe Cullen was
looking for a place to belong.

He understood that, balls to bones. This hotel was
his whole world.

"You ready?" Cullen asked, nodding toward the
front doors. "I got my driver in case we both wanted
a beer."

"You have a driver?" He had a 1984 Jeep CJ-7.

"Well, I didn't until I came here." Cullen waved
over a man wearing a limo-driver black suit. "The
lawyer hired him, and I haven't had a chance to go shop
for an SUV yet."

"Nice to meet you, sir." One hand was held out,
and Matt took it. "Brandon."

"Matt. Pleased."

They shook before Brandon opened the door for
them, getting them settled. "Aspen, correct?"

"L'Hostaria." Cullen sounded so pleased.

Matt ducked his head to hide his grin. Maybe
Cullen was really proud. Matt got the impression that
Cullen had a team to do most of his organizing for him.
Cullen seemed to be ready now to take some control.

"So, have you seen what Neville's people did with
the bathroom in that mini suite?" Cullen asked.

"I haven't had a chance to look at it, no." He was still
spending a huge amount of time on the phone. Cullen had

offered more than once to help with that, but Matt found that Cullen had a real knack with the contractors.

"Okay. Well, pencil me in tomorrow."

He grabbed his phone and made a note. "Done."

"Thanks. I think you'll appreciate the layout."

"I'm sure I approved the blueprints, but I couldn't tell you what the details were." Cullen had come up with the idea of taking two smaller rooms, both tucked into a corner, and combining their two bathrooms into one spa bath.

The Treeline was becoming something special, something amazing. Now, some of the plans Cullen kept trying to show him…. Yikes.

Cullen wanted to make a winter sports arena thing, which wasn't going to work. They didn't need a bunch of twentysomethings there. That led to beer cans and trash, broken furniture, and puke.

"Man, you're thinking hard," Cullen told him.

"Am I? That doesn't sound like me."

"Bullshit. You're more in your own head than any athlete I've ever met. Even this one luge guy…."

"Are they particularly thinky?"

"They spend a lot of time alone going ninety down an ice tube." Cullen grinned, touching Matt's arm.

"I can't even imagine that." And that was no lie.

"Me either. I mean, I go fast, but damn."

"No?" Matt guessed Cullen was into all sorts of speed.

"No. I'll sled on occasion, and we should so go tubing. Luge, though, there are blades there. No way."

"Oh." Matt really didn't know, but ninety and blades and ice sounded… bad.

"Wow. Look at the lights out there." One of the big shopping places in Basalt had decorated up for something, and it did look magical.

"Yeah. Christmas is going to be stunning. So will the Treeline."

"Do you do it up big?" Cullen studied him, vibrating a little.

"We have a couple of times. There've been a few duller years."

"I guess Ben was sick the last couple." Cullen seemed to deflate at that thought. "I haven't had Christmas with, well, not traveling, in years."

"No? That sucks. We'll have a full house and a buffet."

"I like buffets."

Matt knew better, kinda. Cullen had gone from packing in the carbs the first week to drinking protein shakes and running miles and miles a day. Sure, he still put away more calories than the average guy, but Matt could tell Cullen was worried. "We'll make sure there's lots of protein."

"Turkey is good. Lean and mean." Cullen smiled for him, relaxing, fingers still on Matt's arm.

"I'll let Dev know." That was his job, after all. Taking care of the hotel's residents.

"I know I'm a psycho. I just have to start getting ready for the next event." Cullen got a little… distant look in his eyes. As if he were already gone.

"Of course you're not. This is easy. I'm sure it will be no problem." In fact, he'd go ahead and text Dev now with the details so that Cullen wasn't struggling or embarrassed.

"Cool. That makes me feel better about having a big plate of starch tonight." Cullen winked. "So, where did you grow up?"

That change in subject left him blinking a bit. "Outside of Houston. Near Brenham, if you know where that is."

"I think so. It's ice cream, right? There's an old steakhouse on the highway." When he stared, Cullen shrugged. "I like Austin and Galveston, both."

"Ah. Yes. Yes, exactly. I was at UT when I met Ben."

"That's a big school. Lots of competition."

"Yeah, I needed to intern somewhere, and he agreed. I came up here and never left." Thank goodness he'd finished all his course work first.

"I did some classes at CU. A little in California. I kinda wish I'd finished." Cullen picked at his sleeve.

"You have all the time in the world." He turned to Cullen, frowned over. "Don't you like your job?"

"Sure. I mean, I'm good at it." Cullen snorted softly, the sound wry. "I'm just getting long in the tooth for it, and then what? Athletes can be dorks when it comes to the future."

"Ah." What did you say to that assertion? Seriously? He'd known from his first job helping his mom at the Motel 6 that he loved hotels. It was a weird calling, but it was his.

"I know." Cullen leaned toward the window. "Aspen looks amazing at this time of day, huh?"

"It's a fairyland." Very Christmas.

"It is. Sparkly." Only a few moments later they pulled into Aspen proper, and Brandon let them off at the restaurant.

"Text me when you're ready, boss."

"You got it, man. Thanks." Cullen hopped out and waited for Matt, still cute as hell.

He stepped out of the car, the wind cold, the promise of snow on the air. Matt took a deep breath, really feeling as if he was in a whole new world. Cullen grinned at him, obviously pleased, even though Matt wasn't sure why he was so tickled. He smiled in return, then followed Cullen into the restaurant.

The tang of tomato and warm garlic hit him, the yeasty aroma of fresh bread making his mouth water. "Oh, man. I love that smell." He shot Cullen a grin. "I didn't realize I was hungry."

"I know. Like I said. Carpets are the devil. Two for Patrick, please," Cullen said.

"Yes, Mr. Patrick."

"Carpets are not the devil."

"They are!" Cullen made this exaggerated *ew* face. "I didn't even see what was different about the last two we agonized over."

"Philistine! They were totally different." Sort of.

"How? One had swirls and one had… squiggles?"

"Yes. One was maroon and one was more crimson."

"Uh-huh." Cullen winked. "I thought you went to UT."

"Indeed. Note that we went with crimson." He bled burnt orange.

"Isn't that OU?" Cullen teased on the way to the table. "Or no, Alabama. Roll something or other."

"I will beat you." Matt blinked at himself. He never popped off with a tease that way. Never.

"Promise?" They sat across from each other, the table for two in a quiet corner. Nice.

"I swear." Matt knew his cheeks were on fire.

"Woo! Beatings." Cullen fist pumped the air. "Wine? Or do you enjoy beer more? Or cocktails."

"Wine, I think, especially with the pasta."

"Cool. Do you know wine?" Cullen leaned back and watched him, playing with the napkin, the bread plate. Never still.

"I can manage okay," he admitted. "I'm no sommelier, but I know what to serve."

"I'm sucky at it. I mean, I love wine."

"We'll wing it. That's part of the fun."

Cullen shot him a weird glance, and Matt frowned. "What?"

"You don't seem like the wing-it type."

"I wasn't born stodgy." Matt just grew that way, he guessed.

"You mean you can be rehabilitated?" Cullen teased. "Awesome!"

"You're adding to the ass whupping." He wasn't at work right now, right?

"Oooh! You are a Texan!"

"I am." Matt grinned, grabbing the wine list when it was delivered. He wanted a nice, toothsome chianti. There. A Castello would be perfect. Cullen gave him an admiring glance when he ordered.

"That sounds yummy. I love that in Italy. The chianti that comes in pitchers."

"I like wine you can strain through your teeth." He'd never been much of anywhere. Texas, Oklahoma City for an academic contest in high school, and here.

"Italy has some snobbery. Not as much as France, though, because, whoa. But every little osteria has its own red house blend." Cullen shook his head. "I've been everywhere it snows. You know where I want to go, though? Jamaica."

"Yeah? I've heard it's lovely. I have many guests who visit there in the winter." He wasn't going to admit that, at his core, he was a kid trying to keep his head above water. He kept waiting to be old enough where he was the expert, the one who felt as if he was in control, but it hadn't happened yet, so he just faked it. His mom insisted that was the only answer.

"I bet." Cullen leaned in to half whisper. "Sometimes I just want to buy a house and hide for a year."

"Yeah? You should. You can, huh?" It was a free country, and Cullen was famous and shit.

"I guess. I feel like an idiot when I get all picket fencey. Maybe I'm not supposed to have a place." Cullen looked so down all of a sudden that Matt wanted to—what? Hug him?

What good would that do?

"You do have an entire hotel, you know?"

"Nah, that's yours." Cullen said it so casually, so easily, that it jolted Matt to his bones.

The reality of that was, it wasn't true. It was Cullen's, or the Patrick family trust's, whatever. He was an employee. He had more power than most, sure, but that didn't matter. He was still an employee. "That's a nice sentiment, but it's simply not true."

Cullen raised his brows. "Well, you're the one in charge, for sure."

He nodded and let it drop. It didn't do any good to discuss it, and he wasn't going to ever get a better offer, so he'd decided to suck it up and enjoy it.

The wine arrived, and then the waiter poured some for him to taste. Cullen let him do the approving, watching Matt with a tiny smile on his lips. Velvety and rich, he was pleased, and he figured it would go with most all the pasta.

"Do you watch movies?" Cullen asked.

"Sure. I mostly use Netflix and Hulu in dribs and drabs, but I watch."

"What's your guilty-pleasure viewing?"

"I'm a huge monster movie fan—dinosaurs to giant alligators to swarms."

"Oh God. I love sharks." Cullen's eyes lit up. "And yetis."

"Hugeungous ants. Spiders the size of barns." He was totally willing to dish on monsters.

"Ghost ships." Cullen clapped his hands. "Dude, we need a movie night."

"I have a bunch."

"Yeah, and I have a killer TV to break in."

"There you go." The thought of spending a long evening watching movies with Cullen appealed to Matt in ways he didn't want to examine too closely. This wasn't his to lust after, after all.

He didn't want to play that game, did he?

Who was he kidding here? He was really getting attached.

"Hey, you can quit worrying. The hotel is fine without you for a couple of hours." Cullen nudged his foot under the table, and Matt nodded. Better that Cullen thought it was the hotel he worried about than the owner.

"Possibly, yeah."

"You have a great staff." Cullen grinned. "Dev might be jealous that we're eating out."

"He feeds me every other meal, so he'll survive."

"I know! I had this personal chef once. He went on tour with me when Dad thought I was pudgy...." Cullen's expression shut down again. "He got weirdly freaked if I ate anyone else's food."

"That's fucked-up." And he didn't mean the cook. Chefs were weird. He meant the whole pressure thing. Kids didn't need that shit.

Cullen waved a hand in the air. "Prodigies, I guess. What was your favorite thing to do as a kid?"

"Play cowboy." He shrugged and grinned. "And I mean Troy Aikman, not Donnie Gay."

"Football? Cool. College is football, okay." Cullen fidgeted a bit, and if they were at home, Cullen would be drumming on the table, but he was clearly trying to be polite.

"I was a kid." Matt felt funny talking about that, because while he'd been a starting quarterback in high school and a strong second string in his first two years at his starter college, he hadn't ever been under the illusion he was going to be more than he was: a fast, stubborn kid who wanted to play. He didn't even know who was starting for the Longhorns this year, for fuck's sake.

*You're boring him, Matt.* He searched his brain for something to discuss that wasn't sports or the hotel.

He was saved by a pair of teenagers who came up to the table, obviously nervous. "You…. Dude, you're Cullen Patrick. You rock, man."

"Thanks," Cullen said easily, his whole demeanor changing from slightly dork to smooth and smiling. "You guys 'board?"

"Yeah, totally. Like, I can't believe it's you. Trey, here, he's front, like, totally. I'm more the asspass type, but I'm learning."

Were these children speaking English? Honestly? Matt suddenly got it. Stodgy. Okay, so it wasn't all that sudden. It was more being reminded than figuring it out.

"Everyone has to start somewhere. Keep practicing and you'll be shredding in no time." Cullen took the Sharpie one kid handed him and scrawled an autograph on a napkin.

"You rock, for reals." Not-Trey looked at Matt. "Are you somebody, dude?"

"No, son. Not at all." It was his job, in fact, to be no one at all.

"Oh." Disappointment flashed for a moment, but the Trey kid pulled out his phone and took a selfie with Cullen; then both boys were run off by the maître d'.

"What do you want for your starter, do you think?" They had a sweet little selection, and Matt made a mental note to share the list with Dev.

"Something low carb so I can pasta course it up."

"There's a meatball, a salad, olives and cheese…."

"Oh man, I can always go for a meatball. I mean, if a place can't do a good meatball, then why bother?" Cullen grinned, back to goofball in a heartbeat.

"True that. I think I'm going to go for the olives."

"I'm willing to share plates." Cullen gave Matt this look, something warm and happy, and it made his cock twitch in his pants.

Huh.

"I like to share." He refused to blush. Refused to.

"Coolios. Then I say we get the pear and gorgonzola thing too."

"Why not?" Pear and gorgonzola? Hell on a plate, as far as he was concerned.

They ordered it, along with a wild boar meatball and the olive and cheese selection. Cullen seemed so tickled.

When the appetizers came, they were halfway through their first bottle of wine, and by the time the bottle was finished, they were feeding each other olives and bites of salty cheese. He'd lost his mind. The pear was really refreshing, especially after a damned spicy meatball.

This was a hoot.

Cullen laughed as they battled over the last slice of pear, ending up splitting it with a bit of gorgonzola.

"You think Dev can make that?" Cullen asked.

"Yeah, I hope so. I want it for lunch every day." His cheeks heated, and he felt his heart flutter. "Should we order another bottle of the red?"

"Heck, yes. We don't have to drive." Cullen touched the back of his hand, the warmth of the simple contact shocking.

"I shouldn't, but this is our night off."

"It is. We're just two dudes having dinner." Cullen stroked his skin, making Matt squirm.

"That's us. It's been delicious, so far."

"It has. Did we order entrees?" Cullen blinked so comically that Matt laughed out loud.

"Pasta. We ordered pasta and more wine."

"I love pasta." Cullen grabbed a bite of bread, so tiny.

"Have you had polenta? I love that when Dev makes it."

"I have. It's best cooled and chunked up and fried, you know?"

"Oh, yes." He should ask for that, for when Cullen wanted it. Called it in to room service. Whatever.

"I had this thing in Italy once, with polenta and this mushroom ragout."

"Yeah?" He listened to Cullen go on about the food there, the mountains, and he wanted to be able to share his own stories, but they were all normal.

"Tell me about Texas," Cullen demanded, as if it were the most interesting idea in the world. "I've only been to Austin and Galveston."

"It's a whole 'nother country." He hummed softly, shook his head. "There's something special about a place that everyone's so proud of, you know? There's the beach, the lakes, the piney woods. The best part is the people. I miss it sometimes, the easiness of the people."

"That sounds cool. Do you ever go visit?"

"I haven't been home since I left. I haven't been… well, anywhere. This is a full-time sixteen-hours-a-day, seven-days-a-week job. I simply haven't had time."

"Wow." Cullen leaned toward him, eyes bright with curiosity. "Your folks? Are they still around?"

"I never met my father. My mom died from breast cancer when I was nineteen."

Cullen's face crumpled with sympathy. "Oh, that blows. I'm sorry."

"It's okay. It was quick." And it had been brutal. He hadn't even known until ten days before she was gone.

"It still sucks. No wonder you don't go back. I feel that way about Park City. That was Dad's home base. You know?"

"Yeah. I mean, I grew up in Motel 6 in a skanky-assed suburb of Houston. My mom was a housekeeper. I grew up in the hotel business." And this was vastly superior to mopping puke on Sunday morning.

"Wow. I mean, you hear about restaurant kids, but hotel kids? I guess you were a prodigy too. Oh, look at that capellini."

A prodigy. That was adorable. "It smells like heaven."

"So does your risotto." Cullen breathed deep.

"Yes." Okay. Him. Brave. Squid ink. Oh God. Matt swallowed hard, but Cullen saved him by forking up a bite and holding it to his lips.

He opened up instinctively, just pop, parted lips. The squid ink had this oceany but super earthy flavor, and the rice felt soft and pillowy and creamy. So that was totally edible. "It's good. Really good."

"Can I try? I'll share the capellini."

"Absolutely." He shocked himself by forking up a bite for Cullen and feeding it to the man as if he did this every goddamn day.

"Yum." Cullen watched him carefully, smiling, and Matt couldn't care about anything else.

"Yeah. It's good. Hot." *Shut up, Matt. Be good.*

"So tasty." Cullen blinked, long lashes hitting his cheeks, which were flushed.

Matt nodded, reminding himself of all the hundred reasons that this was probably stupid, the main reason being that Cullen was, titularly at any rate, his boss. Still, right now Cullen seemed so young, and so damned cute slash hot that Matt was feeling his oats, so to speak.

That, and the wine was going right to his head. Cullen fed him bites, and they discussed entrees versus getting dessert and skipping meat.

"We should totally have tiramisu with coffee," Cullen said. "Cream and chocolate and rum and espresso."

"Okay, I'm in." He'd bounce off the walls.

"Me too. I want to watch you eat it."

"Cullen." Matt stared, lips open a tiny bit with surprise.

"What? You're amazing." Cullen looked so serious, suddenly. Not joking at all.

"Right. You're famous. You're not worried?"

"Nah. My sport is pretty fluid that way, and I'm really only famous in my sport. Like, our waiter would have no idea who I am if we were in Denver or Boulder. You're totally worth it."

Matt's cheeks felt as if they were on fire. He didn't know where to look, so he just stared into Cullen's eyes.

"You are. I know you're going to tell me it's the wine talking, but you make me feel more at home than anyone I've ever known." Cullen shrugged. "Even when you didn't want to be nice to me."

"I was hurt." He still was, a little, but it was what it was.

"I get that. I mean, I showed up just when you thought the place was yours."

"Yeah, but it wasn't mine." And it hadn't ever been.

Cullen nodded, expression going cloudy. "I—So, tiramisu. Maybe cannoli too."

Matt would pay to watch Cullen eat cannoli. "Yes, please."

"Cool. And coffee. I love espresso." The sunny smile was back.

"Yes." Matt buzzed with the little high from the wine. And Cullen. Cullen made him kinda nuts. Made him ache, balls deep. The feeling was extraordinary for all that it was completely unfamiliar.

They ordered dessert and coffee, and he was going to need some boxes, he'd bet. They finished the second bottle of wine before the sweets came.

"Oh, smell that." Cullen liked to sniff food. Adorable.

Matt leaned down and Cullen lifted up, and the whipped cream covered Matt's nose, little cocoa deposits making him need to sneeze.

"Oops." Cullen rubbed Matt's nose with one finger. "Sorry."

Matt grabbed his napkin, cleaned himself off. "I left a nose print."

"I should totally put that on Instagram." Cullen didn't pull out his phone, though, which made Matt happy. This was for them. Sometimes stolen moments lived longer than anything else.

They each grabbed a fork and started in on the tiramisu, the creamy goodness smelling so good Matt thought he might die. The bite of the cocoa and espresso kept the dessert from being too sweet, but the mascarpone lent a smooth, creamy pleasure when mixed with the whipped cream. Matt closed his eyes and hummed. "Decadent."

"Uh-huh."

He opened his eyes to see Cullen staring at him, fascinated.

"Did I not get it all off my nose?"

"There's a tiny bit on your upper lip." Cullen's gaze arrowed in on his mouth.

Matt licked at it instinctively, and Cullen's eyes went white-hot, a sudden flash of need that stunned Matt.

All Matt could do was sit there, caught by that stare.

It was the waiter that broke their glance, as he refreshed the coffee. "You guys want a to-go box for the cannoli?"

Cullen nodded. "And another order of tiramisu to go, please." At his blink, Cullen just said, "I mean it. I would pay to watch you eat that."

"I was just thinking that about you and the cannoli," Matt admitted. The wine was really doing a number on his inhibitions.

"When we get home, I guess? So we can really watch close?"

Matt caught himself nodding, his moan trying its damnedest to push its way out. "Yeah. Yeah, that sounds…." Well, it sounded as close to heaven as he imagined he'd get, and he wanted it. He wanted Cullen. His body thrummed with his sudden need, and they were both on the edges of their chairs, waiting for the check. It was as if they'd just needed to get out of the hotel for this to explode on them. "Do you have to call him? The driver?"

"I'll text." Cullen whipped out his phone and keyed up a name, then sent a brief note. "He'll be here in five."

"Cool." Matt watched Cullen sign the check, and he reached over, touched one wrist. "Thank you for supper."

"You're welcome. Thank you for coming out with me. I—this is the best night I can remember in so long."

"Yes." And that was that. It had been totally unexpected and wonderful.

Cullen's phone beeped, and they headed outside, boxes in hand. The night air threatened to steal his buzz, but the car felt warm and perfect for a backseat snuggle.

There was a whisper in the center of his brain that he shouldn't, but he was going to, dammit. They were both grown-ups.

Hell, they barely waited for the car to get moving, turning toward each other as soon as they pulled away from the curb. One of Cullen's hands was wrapped around the back of Matt's head even as Matt got ahold of Cullen's waist and dragged him in closer.

When their lips met, it resembled striking a match in the middle of wildfire season. They went right up in flames, Matt's body jumping into overdrive.

Cullen moaned, the sound vibrating against Matt's lips and making him ache with pure hunger.

Matt wrapped both arms around Cullen, wanting to crawl into him, to touch him everywhere. It worked out that he didn't have to because Cullen eased him back and climbed on top of him, rubbing them together.

"Oh. Hey." Matt smiled, hands on Cullen's ass.

"Hey." Cullen shut them both up with a hard, toothy kiss.

Yes. No thinking, no more talking. Matt closed his eyes, letting the kiss transport him someplace magical. He rocked them together, finding a nice, easy rhythm. They had a good little ride back to the hotel. No rushing. This moment was worth drawing out.

He wanted to remember it for years.

Cullen shifted, thighs sliding down on either side of Matt's so no space lay between them. Cullen was solid, heavier than he'd expected, all muscle. Those legs took a lot of heavy hitting against the snow, and the long muscles squeezed Matt, making him grunt and shiver a bit, covered and surrounded.

"Jesus, you make me hot," Cullen said against his mouth. "Hard too."

"Good." It would suck otherwise.

Cullen laughed, a warm, sensual puff of air on Matt's lips. "It is good. So good."

He squeezed Cullen's ass, letting his fingers dig right in and test the muscles. Like a rock. He wanted to see too, but this was not the place. Cullen's cock drilled at his hip through their clothes, and he itched to touch, stroke.

"I want—" Matt cut off the whisper, not sure how to even say it.

"I know, right?" Cullen popped the button on Matt's pants, and his cock popped right out as if it had a mind of its own. Cullen wrapped one hand around Matt's length and pumped him up and down, making his toes curl right up.

Matt decided right then and there that hand jobs were totally underrated. In fact, they might be the best thing ever. The feel of Cullen's calluses against his sensitive skin, the way he could watch Cullen's face, could feel Cullen rock against him. Cullen was hard as hell, their slacks no barrier to their need.

"Here." Cullen proved that the cloth meant nothing by opening up his fly with his free hand, then pushing his cock against Matt's.

"Oh, damn." Matt would have added his grip to Cullen's, but his hands were full.

"Faster." Cullen gasped the word against Matt's neck, pushing their hips together.

"Uh-huh." He was all over that. Matt could totally do faster. They moved, Cullen sort of riding, hand squeezing them so good. The man had great balance. Add his strength to the mix, and they were cooking with oil.

The windows steamed up, the sound of their breathing echoing in the car. Matt knew he was close, the tingles crawling up his spine telling him he was almost there.

"Come on. Please, Cullen." He didn't want to miss this chance. If they got to the hotel, it would be too late.

"Yeah. Just—" Cullen scraped his thumb over the tips of their cocks.

Yeah. Just. Fuck-a-doodle-doo. He shot like a roman candle, as if he was a teenager all over again. When he glanced, he saw Cullen grimace, saw the beginnings of the orgasm overtaking that hot body. He grabbed hold tighter, ground them together, and took a kiss that burned.

"Uhn." Cullen bit Matt's lower lip, jerking madly against him.

It felt dirty, perverse, and wonderful, the way Cullen shuddered and shot. Matt watched every moment, took in every detail he could in the dark car.

"Damn." Cullen rested his forehead against Matt's. "Tell me we can do it again."

"I sure hope so." Matt was going to work very hard to not panic.

"Good, dude, because that rocked my fucking socks."

Matt gave up trying to pretend he wasn't stunned. He took a kiss from that smiling mouth, tasting wine and coffee and chocolate.

"You don't want me to move, do you?" Cullen was laughing, the sound joyous.

"No." And weirdly, he meant it—not from on top of him, but from the Treeline.

He wanted Cullen to stay, even if they did have a lot to wrangle over.

"Five minutes, sir," the driver said discreetly.

"Guess we ought to put the trouser snakes back."

Cullen tilted his head. "Did you just call them trouser snakes?"

"Purple-helmeted soldiers of love?"

"Oh hell." Cullen chortled, the laughter just welling up and spilling out. "One-eyed wonder worms."

"Manmeat. I always loved that one."

Cullen wrinkled his nose, his eyes crossing. "Sounds like something in a can." Cullen grabbed a box of tissues in the little drink console. "We'd better clean up, for sure."

"Yeah. We are a little tom catty, huh?"

"I like it, but what if someone meets us at the door?" Cullen's exaggerated surprise face made Matt snort.

"Yeah. That could be awkward as hell."

"Too true." Cullen dismounted and wiped them clean before zipping up.

"Thank you." Matt meant it too—not about the sex, not really, but about the night. Tonight.

"I get it." Cullen nodded and leaned in to press their lips together lightly.

*Okay. Okay, breathe.* Now was the time to calm down and breathe.

They finally sat back in their own sides of the seat, smiling at each other in the gloom. Matt felt goofy. Drunk.

Maybe a little as if his bones were Jell-O. When they pulled up in front of the hotel, Matt wasn't sure his legs would work.

Of course, when the night manager, Isaac, came out of the main doors, soaking wet and panicked, Matt solidified, flash frozen in seconds.

"What's wrong?"

"Sprinklers went off in the kitchen and the dining room. I need you. Why was your phone off?"

"I was out." Matt shot Cullen an apologetic glance before jumping out of the car. "Show me."

"Jesus, Matt. The kitchen is so wet."

"Kitchens are meant to be washed, honey. So are dining rooms." Thank heaven it wasn't the new ballroom, and the restaurant had those fancy-assed concrete floors and damn the historical ladies. The floor was painted to resemble a fancy rug, which had to count for something.

When Matt got to the kitchen, Dev was directing traffic like a policeman. "No, get that hotel pan out of here. The veg can be washed. The bread is a loss. Right to the Dumpster."

"Hey, Dev. Put me to work." Matt stripped off his good shirt and tossed it in Dev's office, which looked untouched.

"You got it." Dev's scowl deepened. "Nothing was on fire."

"Huh. Let me call Troy. If it's the system, then they can pay for damages, and I need to make sure none of the other rooms get pegged."

"Got it. I'm okay with the evac." Dev winked at him, then went back to marshalling troops.

Matt grabbed his shirt and headed to his office to look at the water sprinkler system readout, already dialing Troy's number.

"'Lo?" Troy sounded a little grumpy, but hey, he had nothing on Dev, whose domain was underwater.

"Matt from the Treeline. There's been a problem with the sprinkler system."

"I'm on my way." Troy was a good guy. Competent.

Matt glanced around, looking for Cullen, maybe. Yeah, no. This was his job. Why should Cullen get all wet and gross?

Cullen was the boss. Matt had to remember that, at least somewhere in his need-addled brain. Forgetting it could ruin everything.

Matt knew he had to do what was best for the hotel. He might be too boring for someone famous like Cullen, but Matt knew what to do with a kitchen sprinkler leak.

That was what he was good for.

## Chapter Seven

**"HEY,** have you seen Matt?" Cullen found himself wandering the halls of the hotel as if he were a ghost in a John Saul story, a little bored and a lot scared that he'd run Matt off with his clumsy fumbling the other night.

When he reached the kitchen, which was super clean and newly dry, he found Dev testing a new frosting recipe.

"Uh. If I had to guess? He's sleeping it off. The damn sprinkler system had to be gutted, and he looks like the walking dead. I swear he's been wandering around the place looking for ghost leaks."

"Heh." No, if Matt had been looking for ghosts, he would have found Cullen. Cullen poured a cup of coffee. "I tried to help with the cleanup, but Isaac ran me off."

"You're the boss, boss. Are you heading up to get him? Because if you are, I have a sandwich for him."

"I'll take it." He'd stop by his little fridge and get the tiramisu. The cannoli was long gone.

"Good deal. I appreciate it." Dev had made Matt a Dagwood; the thing had to be three thousand calories.

Of course, Matt ate maybe once a day.

Cullen grabbed the sandwich, a cup of coffee, and the tiramisu, then made it to Matt's apartment, which he'd never even been in. Quandary—use his key or kick the door?

The key was too hard to dig out, so bang on the door it was. He hated to wake Matt up if the guy was getting some rest, but he wanted to share a sandwich and get Matt to stop avoiding him.

"Coming. Coming. Just a second, guys. Coming."

"Hey!" Cullen grinned when Matt opened the door. "Dev sent a sandwich."

"Cullen!"

The bright smile he got made him tickled as hell, even as he blinked at the exhaustion on Matt's face.

"Shit, I woke you up. I'm sorry." Maybe he should have brought warm milk. "I missed you, though."

"I needed to get up. My days and nights are messed up. Come in. Please."

"Thanks." Cullen slipped inside Matt's apartment, desperately curious.

The place looked like the cleanest goddamn dorm room on earth that had melded with hotel castoffs. Longhorn posters hung over a scarred-up antique desk that must have been worth thousands, and held a huge flat-screen TV. Books and magazines filled milk-crate bookshelves, and the futon sofa was… an abomination, for fuck's sake.

Not dirty. Nothing was out of place. Just—whoa.

Cullen held out the covered plate. "Sandwich. I brought coffee too."

"You rock. Come on in and sit. Let me open the curtains. I was napping," Matt said, and sleep-rumpled was adorable—pillow marks on his cheek and his dark hair sticking up. The heavy stubble surprised Cullen. He'd never seen Matt with so much as a hint of beard.

Sexy. Seriously.

He shook off his paralysis in the face of roughed-up Matt and settled on the futon, sighing with relief when it held his weight.

"You want something to drink? I have a Keurig."

"That would be great. I only had enough hands for one cup." The futon would be okay with some body pillows. Or a new mattress. Yeesh.

"Cool. Dark roast? Breakfast roast? I have caramel latte and hazelnut too."

"Caramel, please." That sounded so yummy.

Matt shot him a happy grin. "It's the best of these."

"Yeah?" Cullen grabbed a chip after he uncovered the sandwich. "Yum. So, the water thing was bad, I guess."

"Shit, yes. We had to keep going from room to room, searching for leaks."

"That sucks. I mean, I had no idea hotel maintenance was so involved. It's like a little town all on its own." Cullen watched Matt's ass move under his sweats.

"It is, especially out here. It's not as if we can just send them next door. It's all fixed, at least for now, and we have guests starting to book."

"That's great! I wanted to help, but the guys shooed me away." Cullen smiled for Matt when he turned around. "I know my ideas seem a little radical, but I'd love to sit down and talk about them."

"This really isn't the place for radical, you know. This is the place for crusty, wealthy folks to rub shoulders with other crusty, wealthy folks."

"Right, but we can keep them mostly separate. I mean, we have the acreage."

"Keep who separate?"

"The hotel and the winter park guests. I mean, if we do that. You know?" Cullen bit his lip. He'd mentioned this to Matt, hadn't he?

"Are you going to try and build a whole separate hotel, then? I mean, I don't know if the infrastructure will hold that. Water, electricity…. The permit process would be insane." Matt brought him his coffee and sat close.

"Cabins, maybe. I mean, a lot of the guests will want to stay at the hotel, and we can get a few shuttles. The cost on that is not bad. Then we could put in a few cabins for guests who wanted large party stays." Cullen warmed to the subject, the idea making him feel as if he could contribute.

"Cabins…." Matt took half of the sandwich. "I can't… I can't imagine having to deal with more buildings, Cullen. I mean, that's huge."

"I know. If I can't figure out how to manage them, we can hire someone. I mean, I think this could bring in great revenue." *Please think about it. Please.*

"I guess." Matt frowned, chewing slowly, eyes on the plate. "I know you think I'm old, but… I just…. This place is special as it is, and I don't want to lose that."

"No. I get that." Disappointment settled in Cullen's belly because he felt this was Matt's place, not his, and he would never do anything without Matt's approval, but he tried for cheerful. "It's just such a great place for winter sports. We're no ski mountain, but a pipe and some speed courses?"

"Yeah. Yeah, it is a good spot." Matt offered him a grin, and Cullen wasn't sure what it meant, exactly. "And you've got the name to bring folks out of the woodwork."

"I do. For now, at least." That awful, squirmy feeling hit him, the one that came every time he thought about retiring. He wanted to, but how long could he ride the has-been name-recognition thing?

"Why for now?" Matt's brows drew down, and he met Cullen's gaze head on.

"Well, I'm not Terry Bradshaw or even Shaun White. Sooner or later my celebrity will fade. I have to retire sometime."

"I think everyone does, really, but you have a long time before you're old hat to the world."

"You think so?" Cullen asked. "I dunno. Any day can bring an injury."

"Sure. I could fall down the stairs or off a ladder. Life sucks."

"I know." Cullen shrugged, not sure how to express what he felt. *Hey, I'm pathetic because I feel closer to you than I ever have anyone on the tour, and I'm desperate to belong?*

Weirdly enough, Matt seemed to be cool with it, just nodding away like it was no big. "I feel like I fell off the earth here, like it's really 1969, and I'm just trying to not mess up too bad."

That made him grin a little. "Yeah. Yeah, I can see that. You're great." Cullen reached out to touch Matt's hand.

"I'm good enough for government work, that's for sure."

"Hey, you're way better than that. Adorable too." His cheeks heated, but Cullen meant it.

"Thanks, honey." Matt surprised him with a kiss, just a chaste one, but a kiss.

Woo. Cullen stole a bite of sandwich, feeling so much better, laughter bubbling up in his chest. "It's good, huh? I love that Dev does that—leaves me food that I crave."

"It's amazing. If I didn't know he was straight as an arrow, I might get jealous."

"Yeah, his philosophy in life is boobies, boobies, boobies."

Cullen laughed out loud, nodding. "More of you for me."

Matt pinked, and Lord, that was pretty—all rosy and pleased. Feeling daring, Cullen took another soft kiss. He wasn't going to pretend he regretted their night out.

"Mmm." He wasn't sure Matt even heard the soft sound of pleasure, but he sure did. In fact, Cullen felt that little moan Matt gave him all the way to his toes. This man had an incredible effect on his libido. And his ego. He was used to being admired for his talent, but Matt was into him for other reasons altogether. Cullen wasn't accustomed to Matt's kind of attention at all.

"I'm fixin' to kiss you again." Matt kissed the corner of his mouth softly. "For real this time."

"Promise?" Cullen grabbed the plates and set them aside, because clean or not, no one wanted to eat a sandwich off the floor.

"Yeah."

Oh. Oh damn. That was the hottest thing in the history of things. Matt slid one hand behind Cullen's head and held him still for a long, slow exploration of lips and tongue.

This wasn't fuddy-duddy or stodgy at all.

No, this was smooth and sweet, a long burn that was going to build.

Matt seemed content to kiss for decades, one after another until Cullen's lips felt swollen. They kinda... flopped down on the couch, Matt on the bottom, and just necked like teenagers. They were both hard, sure, but that didn't seem to be the point. The point was this lazy connection.

When they settled together, mostly petting, not really ramping up, Cullen half expected to be disappointed. All he felt, though, was bliss.

He wanted Matt to touch him, to cup his balls, jack him off, but he didn't want this to stop. Weird. Sex had always been a destination kind of thing. How he got to the end rarely mattered. With Matt, that was the important thing.

Cullen wanted to wallow in it.

Touching Matt might become an obsession. He stroked Matt's flat belly, the skin so soft there, the tiny hairs catching on his fingers.

It probably didn't tickle, but it did make Matt ripple underneath him, shift and moan.

Cullen smiled. Every reaction felt better than orgasms had in the past. Matt made him so fucking happy. It was unreasonable, ridiculous, and utterly wonderful, the feeling swelling in Cullen's chest until there was damned little room for anything else.

Matt shifted, ass sliding on the cushions to bring them together more solidly. That body fascinated him. Matt was no athlete compared to most guys he knew, but he was lean and hard from constant long hours of work. Cullen teased the sweet little six-pack, tickling and playing as Matt jerked.

"Cullen."

He thought Matt might be trying to warn him off in a growly way. That never worked when someone was as breathless as Matt.

"Uhn, you're hot, spread out for me," Matt continued. Oh, he was gonna lose it. Cullen wiggled, trying to tempt Matt into exploring. Matt grabbed his ass, moving them together, putting him right where Matt wanted him.

He stared up into Matt's eyes, trying to figure out what was going on here, what they were doing.

"You make me a little stupid with wanting, you know?" Matt asked.

"I know." He touched Matt's cheek, stroking the sharp line of cheekbone, which was flushed an amazing pink. "Me too."

"You. I mean, I have a bed. It's more comfortable than the futon."

Cullen burst out laughing. "Oh, I hope so. We need to get you a couch."

"I'm not in here enough to worry on it. I'm not a house bunny like you." Matt winked at him.

"Show me your bedroom, huh?" Cullen didn't want to ponder too much how he'd become a bit of a recluse. He'd have to pry himself away soon enough to finish the season.

"I'd be happy to." Matt levered himself up, then held one hand out to him.

Cullen took Matt's hand, curiosity overwhelming him again. He wanted to know everything about this man. Every single thing.

The bedroom was way more… mature? Adult? Whatever. A big platform king bed dominated the space, with two sleek nightstands and a dresser rounding things out. Not really hotel furniture. More midcentury.

"This is nice."

"I bought it with my first paycheck."

"Yeah?" Okay, so when he did get to sleep, the bedroom was a priority for Matt. Good to know. "It's really cool." Cullen didn't sit on the bed, waiting to be invited, maybe.

"Come see if you like the mattress." Matt offered him a goofy grin, looking young as hell. "That was suave, huh?"

"Well, it's as suave as me standing here with my hard-on, wondering what to do next." Cullen took Matt's offered hand so Matt could pull him to the bed.

"We'll get naked and then have mutual orgasms, because those are the best." Practical man.

Cullen tugged off his shirt and sweater. "Okay, now you."

He watched as Matt's lean, lanky body appeared, the flat belly rippled, a tattoo of the state of Texas right above one hip.

"Oh, too cool." They hadn't seen each other at all in the car. That had been dark and crazy. Cullen reached out, tracing the lines: straight, straight, super bendy.

"I was in college. I always wanted a big one."

"I could hook you up." Cullen knew a lot of tattoo artists, somehow.

off the historical ladies. They'd decided Cullen was okay after he'd agreed to fund some sort of restoration of a bandstand in downtown somewhere. Carbondale? Basalt? He had no idea. The Patrick project.

Cullen saw him from across the ballroom and waved, heading toward him as if he was leading a conga line. Matt chuckled, because really, could you conga to "Jingle Bell Rock"?

"Hey!" Cullen said after reaching Matt's side. "How many fires have you put out?"

"Metaphorically a thousand. Thankfully, no real ones. We're packed." Satisfaction lodged in his chest at that thought; 95 percent occupancy.

"Right? This is awesome." Cullen was all smiles, still rocking to the music. "Did we hang mistletoe?"

"Why?" Matt turned when Cullen took his arm, walking along.

"Because I really want to kiss you."

Matt laughed, surprised, but heat built up a little in his belly. "You can't wait until New Year's Eve?"

"Heck no. Besides, I have some kind of thing New Year's Eve. My publicist set it up. It's in Aspen."

Matt stopped, pulling Cullen into the alcove where the ATM and courtesy phone hid. "What? When did this happen?"

Cullen's blue eyes widened. "I didn't tell you. Like, two weeks ago. I won't be gone all night. It's an afternoon thing. I'll be back to help cover the big prime rib thing."

Wow. Matt tried hard not to pop off. This was Cullen's real job, after all. Being a snowboarder. The hotel was just—what? A diversion. And Cullen wanted to build a winter park? Who was going to deal with all that shit when Cullen was back on the road full-time?

"You're mad." Cullen put both hands on his shoulders. "I'm sorry, babe. I'm shit at remembering engagements and stuff. I—it's still new. Trying to tell you about stuff."

"Fair enough." Matt kept his tone even, light, even though the hurt pushed away the happy just a bit.

"Hey." Cullen tugged him in for a hug, which was at once awkward and sweet. "I can cancel."

"No, you can't." Matt gave in and melted into the hug. "It's just Aspen. Promise you'll be back in time for that kiss at midnight, and it's all good."

"I promise." Cullen kissed his neck. "Does that mean the mistletoe is out of the question now?"

"Nope." Matt was so damned easy when it came to Cullen, and he knew it. "I can't let you distract me too much until the party is done, though."

"One kiss," Cullen said. "Screw the mistletoe." That hot mouth closed on his, giving Matt every reason to be merry instead of Scrooge-ish.

No sense in crying over spilled champagne.


**"HEY,** Patrick! You got a minute?"

Cullen had answered his phone on autopilot, and he immediately winced. He'd been avoiding Dan's calls for—well, for weeks. His coach was pretty damned hands-off ever since Cullen had turned thirty, but he had a right to be worried, and to expect Cullen to answer his call. "Hey, Dan. What's up?"

"I just wanted to touch base. I tried to leave you alone over the holidays, but I need to get some idea of what you want to do. I mean, you've been doing your appearances there, I know, so Steve is happy, but are you coming back to the tour?"

"It's too late, Dan. I've missed half the events."

"Yeah." Dan sighed. "Look, no one is upset, and God knows it's not an Olympic year. But you only have so much life left in your knees. I need a commitment for next year soon."

"This whole thing blindsided me, and now I have this thing where I'm gonna put in a winter park here. You know? I have to invest in my future."

"Is that a no?"

"No, that's an I don't know. I'm sorry, coach. I'd love to give you a definitive answer."

Dan paused for so long Cullen thought the call had dropped. "Tell me you're practicing, at least."

"I am." That much was true. He was hitting slopes in Aspen and Breckenridge as often as he could. He'd even gone down to Sunlight Mountain over by Glenwood, which was an adorable ski mountain. "I'm out there a few times a week when I can."

"And you're working out?"

"I put a state-of-the-art fitness room in the basement of this place. You bet I am." The trails were frigid in late December. His balls had tried to crawl up in his body a few times. Snowsuits were so much warmer than jogging layers.

"Good. Should I send Guy to work with you?"

Guy was his trainer, and he would try to kill Cullen for the five pounds he'd put on. "Not now. If I decide over the summer I want to come back, I'll get someone here by July or so." That seemed fair.

"Okay. Well, talk to the rest of the team once in a while too. I actually miss you, kiddo."

"You guys should come now that the season is mostly over, huh? Come see the Treeline. I'm really wanting to get some momentum on this project."

"Sure. Sure, I'll see what I have open."

Cullen had heard Dan say that to a hundred hopefuls over the last ten years or so. It meant "No way in hell, kiddo."

"Thanks. I'm sorry, Dan. I mean, you still have Lee." Lee March was the next Shaun White. Cullen was convinced.

"I do. Hell, I'm getting good money to consult with some of the games popping up like toast. No worries. I just didn't want you to disappear if you weren't good and ready."

"No, I know. I've been buried under blueprints and plans and trying to convince my team to go forward with this." Well, Matt. He was trying to convince Matt. Cullen thought he was akin to water over stone, wearing Matt down a little more every day. The other day Matt had agreed to call some legal eagles.

"Well, holler at me if you want to come to Switzerland."

"I will." Cullen didn't want to go to anywhere right now. He was loving his life.

"Okay. Bye, kiddo."

"Later."

Well, that had been less painful than he'd expected. Maybe he ought to start answering his phone more often.

In fact, when it buzzed again, he hit the green button without even looking. "Patrick."

"Hey, honey," Matt said, voice warm as maple syrup right out of the microwave. "You got time to come taste test Dev's new cookie?"

"I'll be down in three." He needed to do some sprints. Just the thought of leaving those cookies made Cullen sad.

That didn't even touch how he felt when he thought about leaving Matt.


**MATT** hated lawyers.

Hated them.

However, they were a necessary evil. Especially when the owner of the hotel that you couldn't be fired from decided to build a winter park behind said hotel, and you were sort of having a hot and heavy affair with him, so you didn't want him to get in trouble by breaking some strange-assed Colorado law.

So, he'd arranged a meeting with the team of lawyers who dealt with the historical society and the land management people and the state permitting people. Not the estate lawyer.

He hated lawyers.

They were droning on and on about zoning and effective land use and this and that. He didn't care.

What he cared about was if it was legal. If it wasn't, great. He'd tell Cullen. If it was, then they'd figure out the next step in not fucking up Ben's hotel.

Cullen was so enthusiastic. His eyes lit up when he talked about this whole winter park idea and—

"—a special-use permit, but I think it could be done."

"Can someone make a list of what has to be done?" So he could hand it to Cullen.

"Of course. I'll draw that up today and have Lisa e-mail it over." The youngest of the sons, because it was a dad and two sons, smiled at him.

"Good deal. I just want the options clear."

"Of course. There will be restrictions on road use and that sort of thing, so I'll put together a package."

"I'll present it to the owner as soon as I get it."
Every time he said those words, it got easier, and he
wasn't sure if that was sad or just a coping mechanism.

Who was he kidding? Matt liked Cullen too much
to really resent him. They worked well together, and
the personal time—

The more time they spent together, the more they
laughed—over bad monster movies, silly cartoons.
Everything worked. Heaven knew he adored Cullen in
bed. Even couch shopping with the man was hilarious.
Matt wanted to ask Cullen when he was going to have
to leave, but he was afraid to pop the magic bubble
around them. If he suggested it and Cullen decided he
had to go back on tour, it might kill Matt.

"That should do it," the one lawyer said, smiling as
if Matt should know what he'd said before that.

Everyone stood and shook hands; then Matt headed
out, making a beeline for the coffee shop. Snow was
falling, and he admitted that he still got a thrill from
seeing the white stuff coming down. The Texan in him
marveled at the fluffy—not icy—flakes.

He walked into the coffee shop and settled in line,
breathing in the scents of cinnamon and bread and rich
coffee.

"Hey, Matt! How's it going?" The barista's name
escaped him for a moment, but Matt remembered
the kid had worked as a valet for about a month one
summer. Jon. Joe? The name tag read "Jae."

"Hey. Good. Good. How are you doing?"

"Exceptional. Been hanging here, waiting for the
season to open. Is it true that Cullen Patrick owns the
Treeline now? He's vastly crunchy."

What the fuck did that even mean? "Good to know.
Yes, he's taken ownership."

"Wicked. The guy shreds. I mean, he's a genius."

"He is. Can I get a white-chocolate cinnamon latte and a turkey-and-provolone panini?"

"You got it. Is he doing any events? Locally?" Jae rang him up. "Fifteen ninety."

Matt handed over a twenty. "He's going to be training here for a while, I know."

"That's awesome. Cullen is sick, dude. Maybe I can shred with him."

"I… I'm sure he has a Twitter account." Was Twitter still "bitchin'"? Jesus, he was a stodgy old fuck.

"His Instagram is epic."

His sandwich came up at the other end of the counter, so Matt was able to wave and move on. Instagram. Huh. He'd gotten the Treeline a Facebook account, but that was about it. Maybe he needed to talk to Cullen about doing social media.

He grabbed his coffee and sandwich, found a table, and sat, trying to figure out when he was going to stop feeling as if he were an imposter in his own life. How many times had he thought about moving on since Cullen first showed up? Where would he go, though?

And did he want to go? Cullen was… hell, Matt liked him. It was more than the sex. Cullen was the first real friend he'd made since Ben. In fact, Cullen was the same as Ben in many ways, though he didn't know it at all. Funny. Vigorous. Full of life. Matt had tried to decide if that comparison was creepy early on, but he'd finally given it up. This thing with Cullen was what it was.

He stirred the foam into his coffee and pondered his sandwich as if it were a holy relic or some such shit. Maybe he should be proud of himself. Change was hard, but he couldn't be like Ben. He had to allow things to move. To grow.

His phone beeped, Cullen's name popping up with the happy text *it go ok?*

*Fine. Sending email later.*

*Cool. Gotta go practice.*

He nodded—that wouldn't make the slightest bit of difference—and went to check his e-mail. He needed to grab a couple things while he was in town and then head back to the hotel.

Maybe he should schedule a massage. Or a facial. Sheeyah.

Maybe he'd just go buy a new pair of jeans.

Now there was an idea. Maybe he could find Cullen a nice shirt. Something to match his eyes.

He was such a sap.

A sap who was quite possibly in love. His chest tightened with something that felt panicky. No way. That totally didn't work for him. Not at all.

Cullen was a great guy and a heck of a diversion, but he'd get tired of hotelier life and move on. Matt would stay where he was. It was a thing.

He'd never done anything else.

That sandwich wasn't going to eat itself. Matt sighed, then began to nibble. Focus on the important stuff, like his fucking job. The Treeline.

The rest would fall into place. It had to.


**CULLEN** bounced, wanting to do a cartwheel or something. He'd gotten the e-mail from Matt about permits and stuff, and today he'd set a meeting with a course designer he thought Matt could approve of. Yves had created at least three courses at historical resorts in France and Germany and specialized in ecofriendly winter parks.

Excitement rode him, the same feeling as when he was about to hit the pipe. This could be something big, something he could count on for hours, for days.

Maybe years. How cool would that be?

Years here. Years with Matt. The thought should send a spear of panic through him, but God, he wanted that more than he wanted the winter park or a place in the old family business, and he wanted both of those so bad it lit a fire in his belly. Cullen had never met anyone who felt more like home than Matt.

And Matt—well, Cullen was pretty damn sure Matt felt the same way. They could spend hours together and not get bored, and damned if Cullen didn't even enjoy sitting in Matt's office, helping with paperwork.

Of course, he spent way more time watching Matt file and type and deal with the mountains of work than he actually worked. He'd learned to stop chattering when Matt asked him to, and how to deal with Matt's filing system. Antiquated.

Cullen couldn't decide if that was sad or absolutely adorable. He leaned toward adorable because Matt was. Kissable. Suckable. Oh. No wood at a business meeting. Not even for Matt the Hot.

Matt the Sexy.

Cullen chuckled, then almost jumped out of his skin when Matt touched his back, sneaking right up on him. "You okay, babe? Cullen?"

"Sorry. I was in my own little world. They know me there." Yeah, he was defaulting to dork. Great.

Matt grinned wide, the wrinkles at the corners of his eyes crinkling up. "You're excited. That's not bad."

"I am. I think you'll really approve of Yves's design." He wanted to kiss Matt so badly.

"I hope so. I want to do the right thing."

"Me too." Cullen was giving Matt veto power on this. If he saw anything he didn't want, well, so be it. He was fully aware that Matt wasn't totally on board with this whole thing, but he was being a trouper. Really. "Of course right now, I really want to sneak off for a nooner."

These things just kept popping out of his mouth these days.

Matt blinked, but then a slow, happy smile bloomed over his face. "Yeah, I could be into that."

Cullen checked his watch. "Damn. We have to hold that thought."

"We do, but it's a good thought. One to remember." Every so often Matt did something that made him burn, that reminded him that uptight wasn't so bad.

"It is." He touched the back of Matt's hand before they walked to the conference room together.

Yves beamed at Cullen when he walked in, grabbing him and spinning him around in a circle. Weird little Frenchman.

"Uh, hey, Yves. Bonjour. This is Matt Nathanson. Matt, this is Yves Dalmont."

"Your assistant?"

Cullen shook his head. "Nope. Matt is half owner of the Treeline. Everything has to have his approval." He needed to establish that right now.

"Oh, it is my pleasure." Matt got a hug too, and that was damn hilarious. Kinda like watching a three-year-old grab a big cat.

"Uh, thanks." Matt stared at him over Yves's head, eyes wide.

"Let us sit and go over the blueprints."

"Sure."

"Is there coffee?" Matt asked, nose working hard.

"Of course." Yves lifted one finger, and this little guy came in, fawning happily. "Coffees."

Matt chuckled and so did Cullen. Some people loved to serve.

Yves rolled the blueprints out on the table, and Cullen thought he'd just sprung wood. The curve of the pipe... well, it fit with the land around it. Lord, it was perfect.

"Yves, this is... goddamn, dude."

"You like?" Yves clapped his hands. "All the lights will be directed so you cannot see them from the hotel. Solar power. I am so excited."

"Even at night? I love it. I love shredding at night, you know? Especially in the snow. What about backup?" Cullen asked.

"There will be a system in place. I'm working with the county engineers."

Fuck, he couldn't have asked for anyone better. Not a bit. Cullen bounced a little. "What do you think, Matt?"

"I've been looking at blueprints on the Internet. Can you explain how this will affect the soil?"

Yves started into a long discourse about soil samples and testing, and how the balance of nature and man had to remain, and Cullen kinda checked out. He was drooling over this. Now he just needed Matt to give the nod and sign checks.

"That sounds pretty good," Matt said. "Do you have any reports from the similar facility in France?"

"We do." Yves pushed over a tablet with a bunch of pie charts and graphs and shit, and Cullen tried to care, but he only wanted to know one thing.

"When can we start?"

Matt glanced at him. "When I'm sure this is the right design."

Cullen deflated a bit. Matt was on board, he thought.

"We can break ground in April. The main ski areas must be closed for us to get clearance," Yves said.

"So we have time." Matt nodded and frowned. "I don't know enough about this to make a decision right now."

Cullen deflated a lot at that point. "Oh. Well, Yves can send you all of this electronically, correct?"

Yves bobbed his head and then offered Cullen a wide grin. "You should teach him, hmm? How to tell a good pipe."

"I should." Cullen smiled, but he felt stiff, his back a solid block of rock.

Matt looked at him, a long, slow once-over, and then the man shrugged. "Let's do this."

"What?"

"He's the expert. He's the owner. What do you need from us, exactly?"

Cullen glanced back and forth from Yves to Matt. "Yves, can you give us a minute?"

"Of course, *mon ami*. You should have a lunch, *oui*? Meet back at three o'clock, perhaps?"

"Sounds perfect." What a frickin' seesaw of a day. Cullen stood so he could shake Yves's hand.

Matt stood and did the same, dark eyes showing his confusion, his worry. Yves and assistant left them in the meeting room, and Cullen just went right to Matt, then grabbed Matt's hands. "Are you sure? I can wait for you to look at everything."

"I don't know what I'm looking at, and you know it. I know it."

"But I want you to be sure. I'm, like, super impulsive. You're not." Cullen really did care what Matt thought, what Matt wanted. He could suck up the disappointment if he had to.

"I can't be sure. I don't know enough about this to be certain."

"Well, I know a lot, actually, but I can check with this geologist I know on the soil stuff. We can give Yves the provisional go-ahead, but nothing happens until we get the tests?" Would that make Matt feel better?

"It's your land, Cullen. You need to do what you feel is best, and I'll support it. So long as it doesn't ruin what's good about the Treeline, I can't complain."

"I—yeah." What was he expecting? Undying love? Hell, as much as Matt loved that silly hotel, this was a huge vote of trust. He smiled, meaning it. "Thanks, babe."

Matt shrugged, then shot him a grin. "It's important to you, so it's important to me."

Oh.

Oh damn. His cheeks heated, his heart speeding in his chest. Cullen squeezed Matt's hands. "We have a few hours on our own…."

"We do." Matt stepped up, right into his space, bold as brass.

Cullen tilted his head, asking Matt to take this kiss, to show how much he wanted it, and when Matt's lips covered his, he felt the connection, balls to bones. He moaned, wrapping his arms around Matt's neck. He couldn't get close enough.

"Tell me there's a door with a lock. Tell me we can…." Matt looked right into his eyes, obviously trying to be confident, suave.

It was the cutest thing he'd ever seen.

"We so can. No one is gonna say anything." If the door had no lock, he would shove a chair under the handle.

"Good deal." Matt leaned in, lips on Cullen's ear. "I want to suck you off."

Sucking off and getting his pipes? Life was totally going his fucking way. Cullen would have fist pumped, but he had to hang on to his man. His.

Awesome.

"Come on, then. Let's lock the door and make the afternoon memorable."

Cullen dutifully reached for the door. They had a lot to celebrate, for sure, and they might as well start right now.

## Chapter Nine

**THE** pipes were more than half-done, and the snowboard cross course all laid out. Cullen loved the layout of the park, loved the rows of solar panels that marched along the roof of the announcer's stand and the one grandstand.

Yves was a fucking genius, and all Cullen had to do was sign a few papers on this round of contractor draws and wait for the inspector. He'd learned the hard way that there was a hell of a lot of "hurry up and wait" involved in a construction effort this size. A lot of politics.

Matt hadn't thrown him to the wolves, exactly, but he'd made it clear that this was Cullen's baby, and he had to deal with it.

Of course, now Cullen had to go beg Matt to take over the helm of the project for two weeks while he went to Chamonix for a press tour and demo. It might be summer, but that was when people started buying their equipment for the upcoming snow season. Cullen was pretty sure he wasn't gonna compete in the grand prix this year, but he still had obligations. Boards to sign, people to glad-hand. His team wanted him to keep his options open....

"Cullen! There you are, *mon ami*." Yves came trotting up, clipboard in hand. The man had taken a personal interest in this one, for sure, setting up a wee trailer to use as an office. "Can you look at this invoice? I think it is not what we agreed on, and I did not approve an overage."

"Sure, man." Cullen pulled out his little reading glasses and peered. That was new too, thanks to all the computer time he'd pulled lately. "Huh. Let me get my spreadsheet."

He could access all the forms on his phone, which rocked. "We did not approve that, no. Go after him like the rabid French dog you are."

"Arf," Yves said. "Lunch?"

"I'm meeting Matt, but Dev says it's crab salad and croissants."

"Oh, *mon Dieu*." Yves clapped his hands. "He makes real croissant. Not the American plastic. I will go now."

Cullen chuckled, checking his watch. Right. Matt. He hopped in his golf cart once he was at the parking area for the winter park and coasted down to the Treeline, the short drive making him laugh, the wind in his face and his speed probably too fast for safety.

He and Matt were having lunch in his rooms, which seemed silly, that they both still had rooms. They needed to talk about that.

"Hey, babe!" Cullen called out when he walked into his apartment. The place smelled amazing, like garlic and cumin. "What's for lunch?"

"Falafel wraps. Dev gave me the recipe." Matt wore an apron, which, okay, cutest thing ever. He loved that Matt wanted to try cooking for him too.

"Yum. I love falafel."

"Good." Matt took a quick kiss when Cullen got close enough. "Get all the stuff to go with out of the fridge?"

"You got it. How'd it go this morning?"

"Good. Busy. That new hiking, biking, rafting package we put in place is pushing the summer occupancy."

"That's awesome." Cullen rummaged in the fridge, then pulled out tzatziki and marinated onions he found. "I signed off on the next contractor and denied an overage. I feel like God, yo."

"You've been doing too many summer camp appearances," Matt said, dark eyes shining with humor. "Your slang is showing."

"Well, I did keep updating past the year 2000, babe." Cullen plopped down on a stool by the breakfast bar. "Speaking of appearances…."

"Uh-oh." Matt placed a bowl of falafel bites in front of him along with a basket of pita. "What now?"

"They want me in France for two weeks." Cullen opened the tzatziki.

"When?" Matt's tiny frown said more than most people's scowls.

"End of the month."

"Damn." Matt's mouth twisted a little. "Isn't the inspection planned for the cross course?"

"Yeah. Can you fill in for me with Yves?" Cullen held his breath.

"I can, but I really don't want to." Matt held up a hand when Cullen opened his mouth. "I'm not mad, honey, but this is going to be a problem if you have to start doing events this fall. We have a grand opening planned and all. I need you here."

"I know." Cullen chewed his lower lip. "I just— Paul does all this stuff and then calls, you know?"

"I do. You need to take the reins with your schedule if you plan to manage the park. I signed off on all this because you were planning to be here to run it."

That squirmy, uncomfortable feeling he always got when he disappointed someone rushed through Cullen. "I'm sorry."

"Hey." Matt reached out and grabbed his hand. "I'm not trying to be a bastard. I just—well, the Treeline needs you to commit. I want you home too."

Home. That one little word helped deflate the bubble of panic growing under his breastbone. Yeah, this was home. "I'll talk to Paul in Chamonix. I promise."

"Sounds like a plan." Matt filled a pita with falafel. "You're important to me, Cullen. I want you around. I'm not asking you to say you're retiring or anything, but I do want to be in on the plan."

"I can totally do that." Relief sprang up, making him smile. "This smells amazing."

"It does, doesn't it?" Matt's smile was genuine, but there was a watchfulness in his eyes that hadn't been there earlier. "Let's eat. I have a meeting with the grounds guys about the rose garden."

"Roses are nice." Cullen decided then and there that he needed a new spreadsheet to track shit his publicist and agent wanted him to do. Disappointing Matt sucked, and Cullen really hoped he was smart enough to figure out how not to do it again.

**"MATT,** we have a situation down here." Belinda sounded frazzled, but somehow… amused. He knew her barely contained sarcasm voice.

"Where's down here? I'm on the move."

"The front desk. We have that party of twenty."

"Be there in thirty seconds." He ran down the service stairs, three at a time, stopping to straighten his suit and hair before stepping out, going for calm as a cucumber.

Wait, was that a thing?

Cucumbers were cool. Right.

He stepped out into the lobby to see a large group of men and an even larger group of snowboards and travel bags.

Oh dear. "Hello there. Welcome to the Treeline. How can I help you?"

"Hey! Cullen Patrick booked us a bunch of rooms? He said this was a great jump off to Aspen." The oldest of the men held out a tanned, scarred hand. "Jon Dowden. US Olympic trainer."

"Matt Nathanson, pleased to meet y'all. I do have a block of rooms reserved. Do y'all need a common area for your equipment or do you prefer to keep it in your rooms?" They were two hours early, and they were already the loudest guests that had been in his hotel in years.

"Oh, the guys will keep them for now, and once we get to the training facility, they'll leave them. No gross snowboards in the rooms, I promise. However, Cullen mentioned you might want to provide us with a mudroom of sorts for when we get back to the hotel. A place to sort of… become civilized again."

"I'll absolutely make that happen. Let me show you the bar, and Belinda can register you in small groups." He texted Cullen, Dev, and the head of housekeeping, in that order.

Cullen appeared first, trotting down the main stairs, searching for him and nodding once their gazes met.

"Cullen!" The cry rose up, loud and raucous.

"Hey! Guys, good to see you. Jon. Great to have you in!" Cullen pumped Jon's hand. "You're early."

"Yeah, we got a break in the weather. Your manager guy here said he'd deal with us, so that's cool."

"He's the very best in the business." Cullen sounded so confident, so certain, and it warmed Matt's heart.

"Wicked. Who's going to start?"

"Let's do groups of two rooms, and we'll have it done in no time." This was what Matt lived for—solving problems and making people happy.

"Good deal. Can you accommodate us with the restaurant tonight? We have a banquet booked tomorrow, but we'd love to just settle in today." Jon was clearly on the ball with his guys, and Matt approved.

"Of course. I'll make sure the waitstaff knows to reserve the space. Would y'all prefer a number of smaller tables or a single large one?"

"Smaller, I think. These guys can be a nightmare at one big table." Jon winked, and Cullen snorted.

"Totally doable." Matt offered Jon a smile, then headed over to help out on the front desk, making sure to keep an eye on the bar and text Dev again at the same time.

Belinda gave him a bright smile with panic lurking beneath. "Boss."

"Breathe, lady. One room at a time. We're plying them with beer. All is well."

"Okay. That's a lot of testosterone." Belinda blinked over. "A lot of young, rowdy testosterone."

"Be nice," he teased.

"I'm trying, but they make my ovaries hurt."

"You have to watch that. I'm not sure your parts have recovered."

"I know! I'm afraid my uterus is going to fall out."

Matt shook his head. "Too much girl-part talk. Who can we send up?"

"Evelyn says all the rooms are ready, so we need to start at the back and work up."

"Okay." Matt slid behind the desk, watching with one eye as Cullen skated through the crowd.

Together they got the rooms knocked out before Matt had to give away any more than a dozen beers, which boded well for his bottom line. Dev texted him back, and Matt agreed to call in a line cook and one extra server.

He was going to have to discuss adding some on permanently, especially if they added a breakfast or lunch service or kept having good occupancy. Dev could totally manage more staff and keep putting out good food. The man was a fine team leader.

"We have another, what? Eighteen rooms booked tonight?" Matt stretched, his back popping. "Let's make sure that we have something in the lobby tonight—

coffee and cookies by the fireplace. It's going to start snowing again tomorrow, and we'll have more than a few that will need activities, so holler at Yvonne. I'm going to make sure housekeeping does an extra load of towels."

"You got it. Dev has plans for peppermint hot chocolate and some new gluten-free brownies." Belinda winked at him when he rolled his eyes.

"Whatever churns his butter, I guess. I have my phone." And his iPad and his pager, just in case.

"I'm on it." Belinda waved him off.

"Tell me what I can do," Cullen murmured, stepping into stride beside Matt.

"Figure out where to stow all this equipment when it's wet?" That would be the first order of business, and no one was better suited to it than Cullen.

"I'm on it. I think the old carriage area down under the ballroom would work." Cullen gave him a mischievous glance, which told him Cullen had a surprise to spring on him.

"Yeah?" He found himself grinning at Cullen, which was totally not managerial.

"Yep. I'll show you real quick." Cullen took him to the parking elevator. "All the valet guys said the carriage area was nothing but old furniture storage."

"Yes. All the things that didn't fit in my apartment and Ben's old things."

"Well, I didn't get rid of that, but I did organize it, and I think you'll like the new bag storage and valet area so when the weather is bad…."

Cullen led him into the old storage area. Oh. Restored to resemble a place where you'd embark from an antique carriage, there were tons of floor-to-ceiling locking cabinets, a tiled area with safety rugs for people coming in from snow and ice, and a functional seating area where guests could change boots or dry off wet suitcases.

"Oh, look at this!" Matt applauded, tickled as all get-out. Look at his snowboarder-cum-designer.

"I used the budget leftover from the garage, and the hysterical society approved the cabinets and lights."

"And no one called to warn me about you. I'm impressed."

"Well, I did say I was surprising you. If you hated it, I would pay for a new design."

"I don't hate it." In fact, it fit in perfectly while adding value and function.

"Good. So, they can all hump their gear here when it's gross. Jon has assistants who can help our guys store everything."

"Cool." Matt looked around and dropped the fastest kiss ever on Cullen's lips.

Cullen gasped, a pleased sound that made Matt smile.

"Sorry. Just had to."

"I don't mind at all." A flush lit up Cullen's cheeks, and his eyes sparkled.

Matt's phone started buzzing with texts. "I need to get back to work, I guess."

"Uh-huh. I'll go save your lobby."

"Good deal. Thank you for this."

"I totally wanted to do something useful." Cullen patted his butt on the way by. "See you for dinner, I hope."

"If you get busy with your buddies, then after, for sure."

"If I get busy with them, I'll hold out and have a late supper with you." Cullen didn't wait for an answer, which made the statement all the better. Cullen wasn't trying to impress, Matt thought; he just wanted them to spend time together.

That thought gave him a thrill.

He was getting used to this, being a them. A team. Guys who went to bed together at night. It warmed him up, all the way to his bones. The thought of going to bed with Cullen tonight, in fact, would get him through the next few hours. He grabbed his phone as it rang. "Hey, man. What do you need?"

"The bar needs more craft beers, and I need meat," Dev said with no preamble.

"What kind of meat?" If he had to, he'd run to the Whole Foods.

"Lean. Beef and chicken, I'd say. Also we have two vegetarians in tonight, and I don't have enough lentils or tofu. I called in to the Whole Foods. You just need to send someone. Sorry, Boss, I was on a strict budget thanks to this banquet tomorrow."

"No sweat. You know that you just have to let me know. Is there enough to feed them in the morning?"

"Yeah. Eggs I have. I was planning to test my new baking assistant with meringues, but we can wait on that." Dev sounded amused now.

"I'll have the order delivered. No worries." Matt grinned, shook his head. "We have eight reservations for tonight on top of the party of twenty. That should be fun."

"We got this. Just get me the food." Dev hung up and Matt nodded. Right. Time to do magic.

Lord, he loved his job.

## *Chapter Ten*

**CULLEN** bobbed his head to the music, grinning while he watched Aaron Lee breakdance in the center of the ballroom. Dork. Lord. The party was going good—Dev had outdone himself with munchies, and the acoustics and lights were great. The guys were tearing up the dance floor, and thank God the ballroom sat back away from the guest elevators.

The service doors opened, and Cullen saw Matt, still in his official GM suit, carrying another tray of goodies.

Cullen made his way over so he could grab the tray. "Hey, babe! Can you hang out?"

"This is the last bit of munchies." Matt smiled at him, and Cullen thought that Matt wanted to stay.

"Oh, good. I mean, the guys would love to meet you, and if you could stay a bit—" Cullen stopped short of batting his eyelashes.

"I need to change. I'm overdressed."

"If I let you leave, you'll never come back." He took Matt's arm, leading him to the drinks.

"Listen to you." Matt looked pleased, grinning at him and blushing.

"I know, but it's true. You're dedicated. It's late. The hotel can run at night for a bit without you."

Cullen eased Matt's suit jacket off and stowed it on a chair back in the corner, and when Matt removed his tie and unbuttoned the top two buttons of his shirt, Cullen found himself springing wood. Woo, his man was sexy. So not staid and buttoned up now. "Come dance with me?"

"Your friends won't be pissed?"

"Nah. Half of them are the kings of bro jobs." Cullen winked when Matt cracked up.

"I love dancing."

Oh, that was good to know. "Excellent. Then we can gyrate together."

"No two-stepping?" The words were a tease because Matt moved up against him, body moving like a wet dream.

"You could teach me. I know how to waltz."

"This isn't a waltz. Maybe later."

"No, this is vertical foreplay." Cullen put his hands on Matt's hips, then tugged their bodies together.

"Yeah. I could learn to be into this."

His blood heated up in his veins, and Cullen's heart began to pound. "Me too. I really could."

Matt nodded and rocked toward him, sliding one leg between his, so daring. So not stuffy. They swayed and shuffled to the beat, both of them breaking a sweat. The beat was driving them, and Cullen's cheeks hurt from smiling. This was as good as a really amazing run, burning a three sixty and landing it easily.

He hadn't thought anything else would feel so good, but he'd been so wrong. Matt was the best thing to ever happen to him.

Seriously.

Matt was… his magic, his own personal high.

Cullen leaned against Matt a little harder. "We could go party alone."

"Do you want to? I'm right there."

"I don't mind showing you off at all," Cullen said. "But I want X-rated things."

"Then we should head upstairs. My place or yours?"

"Mmm. Yours. I like your bed better." Cullen took Matt's hand, feeling brave.

"So long as it's not my futon, hmm?"

"Hell, no. If it wouldn't offend you, I would buy you a real couch." They were going to go shop for one at some point. He was determined. Even if he had to get Matt a reupholstered antique.

A tiny voice inside him whispered, *Maybe we could put it in our apartment.*

"Let me grab my jacket."

"Okay." Cullen was feeling loose, agreeable. Jon boogied by, waving at him, and he caught the man's eye. "Hey. I'm heading out. Keep them in line, will you?"

"Right. They're just playing. That one yours, or is he up for grabs?"

"Mine. All mine." Cullen tried a smile, but he would bet it came off as more a baring of teeth.

"Rock on. Nice catch, dude. He's a class act."

"Thanks." Now Cullen did grin, beaming at Jon. "I think so."

He felt Matt's gaze on him, knew it wouldn't take much for Matt to move from wanting to worrying. He waved at Jon again and headed over, bouncing to the music. "Ready, babe?" Cullen asked.

"I am. Everything okay? Do they need anything?"

"They're good. Jon wanted to know if you were single." Cullen grabbed a wee plate off the goodie table on the way out, then filled it with an assortment of finger food.

"Me?" God, that confusion was cute.

"Yep. You're a total hottie, babe."

"Right. I believe the word you used was stodgy. Utterly stodgy."

"I did?" Cullen tried for innocent. "Well, you do loosen up a lot when someone gets to know you."

"Yeah, I do."

He had to admit that it felt fucking amazing that Matt was willing to let it go, to give it up without a big drama thing. They'd worked hard over the last weeks to get to this place, to know each other well enough to be able to tease and talk and agree.

Matt took him out through the back hallway, leading him to the second floor. "The main lobby is going to be full of people who will decide they need something."

"Oh, good man. So smart." That meant he could feel up Matt's butt.

"I've been playing this game a long time. A decade."

"Uh-huh. How many times have you actually gone up the back way?" Cullen would bet not many.

"A couple. Once when this guest wanted to buy my services. She was ninety-two and rather… insistent."

"Oh, you dog! Getting granny all hot and bothered." The very thought was hilarious.

"I felt bad for her, but… not that bad."

"No, I guess not." The whole idea was kinda *ew* when you took the funny out of it.

"Still, it made me think of those old cartoons." Matt opened the door to his apartment. "Come on in?"

"Uh-huh." Cullen scooted past Matt, then grabbed his lover's hand and pulled him inside, as well.

Matt let the door shut behind them, and they stood there in the dark, the moonlight bright enough off the snow that they could see each other, the dark shapes of the furniture. Cullen took the kiss he really wanted, grabbing Matt's ass and hanging on. His lover moaned, the sound welcome and unbearably wanton. When had he ever thought he would use that word?

"Did you know I just used wanton in a sentence in my head?"

"Did you? I approve. I just used utterly fuckable."

"Oh." Cullen blinked, then swung Matt in a circle. "Let's see what other words we can come up with."

"Works for me. I think we should go alphabetically." Matt's hands landed on his ass. "I'll start."

Cullen nodded, gazing into Matt's eyes. "You're the brains."

"And you're the boss. Come to bed."

Cullen let Matt lead him to bed, and he hoped this was how it would be forever. He didn't think too hard on how he would make that happen. He just went with it for now, as he did when he let the powder tell him which way to go.

Sometimes you had to trust your gut.

**MATT** woke up to his alarm buzzing insistently, and he slapped at it. *Shh. Happy. Warm. Naked. Shh.* He nuzzled against the nape of Cullen's neck, his body pleasantly sore and comfy.

"Mmm, babe." Cullen turned toward him, draped an arm around his waist, and pulled him close. "Sleep."

"I can't, honey. I have to get up and get to work." He wanted to stay. So bad.

"You need an assistant. We need a day to snuggle."

Snuggle. If he stayed here, he would be riding Cullen like a prize pony. They had this incendiary chemistry, and Cullen really was an amazing athlete. All stamina.

"I have to go to work, honey." He kissed Cullen's temple, then levered himself up off the bed.

"I am now bummed." Cullen flopped to his back, arms and legs spread dramatically.

"Oh God, me too." He wanted a piece of that, so bad.

"Well, I guess the guys will be looking for me." Cullen pretended to be grumpy, but his eyes twinkled, the humor clear as the sun outside the windows, shining off the snow.

"Yeah, they want to see the champ do his thing."

"Nah, they just want me to wipe out." Cullen rolled out of bed.

"Could be a fun day."

"You should come. Strap on a board."

Oh, there was no way. He didn't know how, and he had work to do. "I wish I could."

"Well, you'll have to come out at some point. The guys will want to show off."

"I'd love to watch, sure."

"Cool." Cullen came to give him a kiss. "We'll meet back here tonight, if nothing else."

"You know where to find me."

"I do. Hard at work." Cullen pinched his butt but let him dress and head out to work with only one more kiss.

Matt made it down the stairs, almost, before Yvonne grabbed him.

"There you are!" She smiled at him, handing him a huge folder. "The coach guy. Jon? He had a bunch of dates he wanted to talk about, and about bulk discounts."

"Excellent. Did you work it up?"

"I did, but you need to sign off on it for me." She grimaced. "Just in case, you know?"

"Hey, breathe. It's all cool." It was good, wasn't it?

"This is just more than I'm used to, Boss. I don't want to screw up."

"Neither do I. We'll have to not screw up together."

"That's the best way. Dev was looking for you too."

"I'm heading for bagel and coffee. I'll find him as soon as I check in at the front desk."

"Good deal." She waved him on. "Holler at me when you've had a look."

"Will do. Give me an hour." He headed down to the front desk, his brain finally switching into work mode. Coffee was definitely paramount. Matt detoured to the kitchen before the front desk. "Hey, Dev. How's it going?" He made a beeline for the coffeemaker.

"Good. You check in with the desk? I know Isaac left a couple of notes."

"I haven't, no. I need coffee. I'll head right over."

"Coffee I got. Mexican latte or caramel hazelnut?" Dev was a god.

"Caramel hazelnut. God, you're a good guy."

"I so am." Dev gave him a sideways look while steaming milk. "Good night last night?"

"Yeah. Yeah, it was." He got a weird niggling feeling, and he tried to catch Dev's gaze. "Is there a problem?" It wasn't like he was in the closet, really.

"What? No. No. You have Isaac for a reason. You just split pretty quick last night, I guess? Folks were looking for you."

"I'd been working for fourteen hours, and I had a great offer. I was in my room. I was available for emergencies." Dammit.

"Hey, I'm not judging. I'm just letting you know you might get some looks." Dev handed him a plate of pastries instead of his bagel. "Bagel is toasting, but the front desk crew would love these."

"Sure. I'll be back in a second." He took the tray and headed out, trying not to growl. He didn't have to fucking ask the staff's permission to have an affair. His shoulders rose up around his ears, and it took everything in Matt to smile at Rosa, who was cleaning the entryway windows.

"Mr. Matt. *Buenos días.*"

"Good morning, lady." He held out the tray, offering her a bear claw.

She took one and slid off to the side of the lobby to munch on it. Yeah, time was the enemy all over the hotel.

He took the tray up to the front desk. "Hey, guys, good morning."

"Morning, boss." Belinda grabbed a cherry turnover. "Must have been a crazy night."

"Yeah? What happened?" *Goddammit.*

"A few noise complaints. One inquiry this morning about when the large party is leaving. Mr. Arnold said, and I quote, 'I come here to get away from those people.'"

"I'll speak to him." But what was he supposed to say? If younger guests didn't start coming, how would they make it? If the snowboarders didn't stay here, would they use Cullen's pipes?

He didn't want to lose customers like the Arnolds, but there had to be a happy medium.

"Cool." She lowered her voice. "Personally, I think he's a sourpuss. Isaac says the guys were really good, actually. The Arnolds just had their windows open."

Hell, they might have heard him and Cullen…. The thought made Matt's cheeks heat, but he was not going to be ashamed. He was an adult, and so was Cullen.

"Oh ho! Your chin just jutted. Stubborn Matt to the rescue." She winked at him, cheerful as anything.

"I don't know what you're talking about." He did wink back at her, playing and keeping it light. "Should I leave the platter up here, do you think?"

"Yes. And tell Dev to send more." She waved at her more ample figure. "Still eating for two. Or three. Maybe a whole village."

"Right on. I have to grab my coffee, and then I have a proposal to go over in the office. Call if you need me. My phone's charged."

"Will do. Oh, and Kyle down in maintenance wants to chat with you about the heaters at some point."

"Can you please send me a text to remind me?"

"You got it." She held up her thumbs, weirdly nude of her acrylic nails. Belinda said they were too hard to maintain, with the baby.

Okay, back for coffee and bagel and to see why Dev's feathers were ruffled. The big guy rarely snarled, and when he did, it was always so subtle, as it was this morning.

His bagel had burned. Matt smelled it as soon as he walked back into the kitchen. A new one sat in the toaster, waiting for him to arrive to toast to order. So. Dev wasn't pissed at him, just at something.

"You're the hero of the front desk." Matt leaned against the counter, offering Dev a smile for his coffee. "You ready to tell me what's up?"

"Well, I need to know if we're planning to be this busy from now on." Dev wouldn't look at him, really. Those heavy dark eyebrows pulled down into a scowl, and Dev began chopping veg.

"I hope so, yeah. It's going to be how we make this a going thing." He'd spent a lot on the remodel, and he intended to recoup those costs.

"That's cool, but I could do this mostly alone when we were a sleepy, old folks' place. If we're gonna be happening, I need something more than temps, you know? I never work with the same sous or waiters twice around here with all the resort competition. And I want to hire this kid I know as my chef of room service. I got three plates sent back last night because the guy I assigned sent up prime rib nicked from the banquet rather than a cooked-to-order steak."

"Okay. Hire him." And he needed the name of the guy from last night to put on the do-not-hire list.

"Seriously?" Dev was suddenly all smiles. "What kind of salary can I offer?"

"Start him at thirty-six, meals here. Fair?" Matt made some notes on his phone. "He'll have to work some long hours until we can justify another line cook, so make sure that's clear."

"You got it. Angie says she can do part-time pastry, so that will help me, though I do love to bake." Dev handed him his bagel. "Thanks, Boss."

"You know I got your back, man. Thanks for the breakfast, by the by."

"No problem. I got more pastry for the paying guests if you want to send someone down to haul it to the desk."

"Will do. I'm heading to my office. Holler if you need me."

"You know I can yell loud." Dev began bellowing some song about shots, wiggling his butt in time.

Okay, that was obviously his cue to get the fuck out of Dodge. He backed away, texting this person, calling that one while making his way to his office and eating.

Crap. Matt texted Dev to get the name of the cook to go in the no-interview file. Sometimes he forgot his own brain.

Before he knew it, he was lost in his work, lost in the day-to-day, the steady rhythm.

The phone jarred Matt out of his spreadsheets about two in the afternoon, and his stomach growled.

"Matt, how can I help you?"

"Hi, there. I have a guest who would like to speak to you. Can you come to the front desk?"

Ah, shit. Belinda had her teeth-gritting voice on.

"I'll be there in two shakes." Matt grabbed his jacket and a peppermint—breath freshening and a nice pick-me-up—and made his way to the front desk.

Mr. Arnold. Rats. Matt had really hoped to take on the old dude on his own time and with some preparation. "Mr. Arnold. How can I help you?"

"You know that I have been a guest at this hotel for forty years?"

"Yes, sir." Old goat. Matt forced himself not to roll his eyes. Ben had thought Mr. Arnold was, what did he call it? A snoot. He kept that in mind.

"I have never had an experience as I did last night. Those people were so loud."

"I'm sorry, Mr. Arnold. Perhaps instead of your usual room, we should book you in the east wing. You're close to the ballroom, unfortunately."

"Is that area renovated? I wouldn't be averse to a new view."

"It is. It's quite lovely and a bit quieter, and the morning sunshine is glorious." The old guy was pissy that his regular room had just gotten a standard reno, Matt would bet. He thought he deserved fancier for his long-time money. Matt could totally give him that.

"You'll send a bellman for our things."

"Of course. Is an hour sufficient time for you?"

"It is. Thank you, Matthew. I knew once I could speak to you, our situation would be handled."

"Of course, Mr. Arnold. You're one of our most cherished guests. Belinda, let's move Mr. Arnold to the Olive Suite."

"Yes, sir. I'm on it." She hid her smile behind the computer screen.

"Thank you, Matthew. I appreciate your understanding."

"Of course, sir." It didn't take more than respect and listening sometimes to ease tensions and take people out of defensive mode.

Mr. Arnold swept off, presumably to pack for the move, and Belinda grinned hugely. "Good one, Boss."

"It's my job. Get hold of housekeeping and have someone zip over to that room, and make sure a bellman is standing by."

"I'll call Serena. She's in that wing." Belinda grabbed the walkie-talkie, and Matt headed to the kitchen. He needed another miracle from Dev.

"Dev? I need a little don't-be-pissed-off platter. Think seventy-year-old not romantic, in forty-five minutes."

Dev paused, knife hovering over Romanesco. "The Arnolds?"

"However did you guess?"

"Oh, I dunno. Maybe it was the wildfire spread of doom and gloom. Glooom! Whatever will we do without the old guard?" Dev batted his eyelashes and held his chest as if he were having a heart attack. "We'll get to cook food that people can chew, that's what."

"You're an ass. I adore you. Is there something I can steal for lunch?"

"Chicken salad wraps are in the fridge." Dev handed him a plate. "Get some of the three-bean stuff too. I need a taste tester."

"I can do that." He fixed himself a plate and sat in the kitchen, checking his e-mails again.

"Breathe." A new cup of divine-scented coffee appeared at his elbow.

He looked up at the guy who had honestly become one of his best friends on earth. "Yeah?"

"Yep. I mean, some of the staff is freaking out, but I think it's more like one of those bar or restaurant redo shows. They're not used to being this full up."

"It's looking up, isn't it? That's good." He loved this hotel with a passion, and he wanted it to succeed more than anything.

"It is. I'm proud of what you've been doing." Dev grinned at him, then began pulling out strawberries and chocolate and weird little breads.

"The salad is nice—a little sweet, a little sour. Very nice."

"Yay. I hate how sweet most of them are, but I can always add a little simple syrup for the more traditional set."

"Are you going to start having old people menus on the side?"

"Nope." Dev chuckled, the sound vibrating around the room. "I'm just going to have one menu I can tweak to suit any guest."

"You're a good man. Are you set up for the banquet deal the snowboarders are putting on day after tomorrow?"

"I am. I got the order in, and the delivery comes tomorrow morning. I picked my servers and all, and with my new cook, I'll be golden."

"That's what I want to hear. I have a couple of guys coming up to move tables and chairs for us too."

"Good deal." Dev rummaged in a jar, then handed him a cookie. "White-chocolate macadamia."

"You're going to make me fat."

"Shit, as much as you run? I couldn't." Dev whirled and chopped and flourished, and a plate appeared, filled with dainty treats. Dev hit the intercom to the bell desk. "I need a runner for a suite-welcome plate."

"On my way," one of the servers called back.

"Okay, I have a meeting. Yvonne made a good deal with the guys—repeat guests are happy guests." Matt didn't wait for an answer; he waved and headed out, a bounce to his step and a smile on his face.

He could do this. They were doing this.

## Chapter Eleven

**"YOU'RE** moving slow, old man," Sheney Thompson told Cullen, clapping him on the back on the way by.

"I haven't been on the slopes and pipes enough, for sure." Cullen grimaced, surprised at how sore he was after a day out with the elite boarders Jon had brought with him. One too many beefed runs, the last one crashtastic enough he was lucky to be walking.

"Yeah. You worked it, though, and it was a total bluebird up there."

Cullen agreed. The day had been amazingly beautiful and the snow crunchy as hell.

"Mr. Patrick? Cullen!"

Cullen put on the brakes, swerving toward the front desk, where Lianna, the clerk, waited for him. "Hey! What's up?"

"You have a message." She grinned at him and passed over the envelope with a stylized *C* scrawled over the front.

"Oh." He stared at it, kinda afraid to open it. He knew that handwriting. Hell, he'd broken up with it well over a year ago. "Thanks."

Tony was an advertising exec—big power, big money, big gestures. Just the thought of the crazy fucker made Cullen tired. Oh, yeah, Tony was charming, very continental, even if Cullen knew he was from Tahoe.

He tore open the envelope, half afraid a snake would pop out and bite him on the nose.

> *Hey, babe. Joe invited me out.*
> *Saw your name. Had to come. Owner*
> *now? Moving up in the world. Let's*
> *hook up. Miss your mouth. T.*

Cullen glanced around to make sure no one had— what? Heard the letter as if it was some sort of Harry Potter movie he lived in? His cheeks felt hot, and he cleared his throat. The pure balls it took Cheating Tony to call him babe and mention his mouth as if he had a right to it left him speechless with something close to rage.

His phone beeped, and he almost didn't check his texts, but he did and was glad for it. Matt was outside— maybe on the roof?—and there was a picture of him in the snow, red-cheeked and grinning.

Cullen tossed Tony's note in the trash and texted back. *Where R U?*

*Heading to the snowmobiles to make sure they're all good to go.*

*Be right there.*

Suddenly he wasn't at all sore anymore. Matt's bright red coat was a beacon in the snow as his lover waited for him. Cullen charged up the hill to the shed, grinning like a fool. Matt just made his heart happy.

"How was the pipe?" Matt grinned at him, dark eyes resembling buttons in a shirt.

"Crunchy. Awesome. I fell on my ass a damned good bit." He would have to show off his bruises later. In private. "Good day?"

"Yeah, it was. I got stuff done."

Cullen knew Matt enjoyed that. Just getting all the things accomplished.

"Good deal. You want to go for a ride?"

"Yeah? You up to it?" Matt lit up like Christmas.

"I totally am." He tugged a protein bar out of his zipper pocket on his pants. "Let's do it."

Matt clearly caught sight of the wrapper. "You need food?"

"Babe, I need to zoom out there with you more. We can eat when we get back." Plus, this way he could avoid Tony until his ex went to supper in Aspen or someplace equally fancy.

"If you're sure." Matt unlocked the shed and stole a quick kiss. "Hey."

"Hey." Cullen stole one back, just because he could, Matt's lips cold as the snow.

"You want to ride together or take two sleds?"

"Oh, you can drive." He waggled his eyebrows, but he did want to see how Matt handled a machine like this.

"I can."

Okay, so that confidence was fucking sexy as hell. Cullen munched his protein bar quickly, feeling it hit bottom. *There. Fed until they got back. Quick calories.*

Matt checked the sled over, texted someone with their plan, grabbed a snowsuit, and pushed the snowmobile out the door.

"Man, you know your shit with these. Why have you never learned to ski or snowboard again?" Cullen asked.

"I have my motorcycle license. This was easy. Skiing is a skill that I didn't learn before I was a hotel GM."

"Ah. Well, I bet you have skills here." Cullen tugged on his gloves and climbed on behind Matt.

"I do." And like a boss, Matt got them moving, slowly until they were out of range of the hotel, and then zipping them through the trees fearlessly. The wind stole Cullen's breath, and all he could do was hold on and let Matt take him for a ride.

Cullen whooped when they hit soft snow and Matt burned the fuck out of it, not letting them sink one bit. They shot up out of the hollow and over a little rise, and whoosh—they swooped down a hill, two kids on an out-of-control toboggan.

Jesus, he'd thought this man was stodgy? No one drove this way if he was scared. This was adrenaline, pure and simple.

Matt cackled, a noise the wind stole and threw past Cullen's head. Like a big bird. The sound made him laugh out loud.

They had to have been out for an hour when Matt parked them under a tree, the hotel a gorgeous red-roofed monstrosity nestled up against the mountains. The pipes were right there, where they were meant to be, fitting in naturally.

Cullen hugged Matt's waist. "You are a stud, babe."

"Thought you'd appreciate the view."

"This is amazing." Cullen shut off the voice in his head that said they should offer snowmobile tours of the pipes. This was not the time for business. Instead he pressed his cold mouth to the line of skin just under Matt's hairline.

"Mmm." Matt leaned back and rested hard against him.

"What a beautiful day." Happiness bubbled up in his chest as if someone had shaken a champagne bottle.

"It is. Crisp and clear." Matt turned his head, begging another kiss.

Cullen gave it, feeling weirdly daring right out in the daytime, kissing his lover. He was really starting to feel that this could be his future, and he had a place and someone who cared. Matt and the Treeline, they could be home.

Matt stroked his cheek with a gloved hand. "You ready to go get some supper?"

"I am. Thank you for this." For all of it.

"Thank your grandpa. He built it."

"No. I mean, yes, but you kept it going. And you're you." He hushed Matt with another kiss. Matt opened up for him, easy as pie. They were making out on a snowmobile. How frickin' cool was that? Cold as he was, Matt's kisses warmed him deep inside.

"Let me take you home, Cullen. I need to feed you."

"Okay." Yeah, his stomach was rumbling, and not with happy horniness. "Home sounds good. Maybe a nice hot shower."

"Maybe a nice hot toddy."

"Oh, I bet Dev would do that if we texted him from the shed." Cullen loved a hot buttered rum.

"It's a plan. You want to drive home or should I?"

"Oh, I want you to. Unless you're pooped. You're way better at it than I am."

"Works for me. Let's go." Matt was all smiles as he started the engine up again. Cullen held on, the hill working his abs hard as they went up instead of down. Fuck, that was a hellacious grade.

Still, Matt drove like it was nothing, getting them back to the shed lickety-split. They went through all the steps of sled maintenance, and then Matt texted Dev. Whatever he was asking for, it was more involved than just hot toddies.

He had to admit it warmed him, how Matt took care of him. Oh, Matt took care of everyone, but Cullen seemed to be a special case, and he wasn't going to complain. They slipped and slid down the slope to the hotel, holding on to each other for balance, laughing out loud.

Matt got their snowsuits off in the area he'd created for the snowboards. Cullen was tickled to see it worked so well. There was an alcove to hang up the wet snow gear, with extra heater vents to keep a guy warm while he dried out a bit. Cullen was a little ashamed he'd clomped through the main lobby before, not even thinking about it.

It was all a learning experience, right? Right.

He took Matt's hand when they hit the elevator, happy to just hold on. "Man, that snow is sweet."

"That snow is cold, but yeah, I hear you. That was the most fun I've had since last night."

"Last night was a different kind of fun." Cullen's cheeks heated, and parts of him he thought were frozen perked up too.

"Last night was the best kind. Let's get you fed and warmed up."

"What did you ask Dev for?" The elevator dinged, and they let go of each other, a loss Cullen actually felt as a physical blow. He was clingy tonight, dammit.

"Just a snack for us to share." Matt looked utterly pleased with himself.

"Yeah? You're good to me." They skirted the lobby, skulking along the back hallways to the kitchen. Cullen was grateful that no one stopped them, because his hands were shaking with the need to eat.

Dev had the table set with a bunch of savory and sweet goodies, along with two hot buttered rums. Oh, dude. The man was a king.

Cullen grabbed a chocolate-dipped strawberry and a tortilla roll up, stuffing one after the other in his mouth. Oh, good. Okay, he could slow down any minute.

Matt drank his rum, eyes on Cullen, expression warm and fond.

A man could learn to live for that expression. Cullen wanted nothing more than to be right there with Matt and run their hotel and be just a guy. Holy hell, was that even possible? Could he do that? He'd have to talk to his sports agent about the sponsorships, see if they even wanted a retired snowboarder to do their energy drink spots....

He had his money, and Grandpa's money, and....

What was he thinking? An innkeeper? Running a pipe? Matt might be playing house, but was he really wanting to settle down with the new owner?

Matt licked a bit of chocolate off his finger. "Man, that's yummy."

"Uh-huh. Good. Is that a crab puff? In Colorado? Dude."

"Dev's a miracle worker."

"I am." Dev came by and grabbed a cookie. "Tax for eating in the kitchen."

"We'll eat supper upstairs, unless someone has an emergency or Cullen's made other plans."

"Nope." Cullen felt so much better, and he sipped at his drink. "I save my evenings for you."

Matt's cheeks went a warm, bright red, and his lover looked as pleased as punch. The pendulum swung the other way, and Cullen knew what he was thinking. He was thinking he couldn't give that up.

"You two are adorable. Get out of my kitchen." Dev offered them both a wicked grin.

"Send up dinner?" Matt said. "My rooms."

"Already arranged. Go. Be naked together."

Cullen almost swallowed his tongue, not used to the easy teasing on that front. Still, it felt good not to worry or hide. Dev was family now.

"Listen to you." Matt stood and grabbed the platter. "Get the drinks?"

"Got them." Cullen tucked two bottles of water into his deep pockets before he picked up the tray, because they would both need it.

They headed through the lobby to check with the night manager, really quickly, and Cullen found himself praying for no problems.

"Cullen! There you are." A perfectly coiffed man wearing Eurotrash jeans and Italian loafers trotted across the lobby toward him. Shit. Cullen had forgotten Tony.

Matt put the little tray down, answering a question about room rates.

Might as well meet and greet and be done. "Hey. Tony. How's it going?" Cullen shifted from foot to foot, impatient.

"Good. Good. I was excited to hear that you were going to be available. You've been on my mind, quite a bit."

"Yeah?" What the hell did Cullen say to that? Tony was still pretty, with his tight curls and bright green eyes, but the hardness around his mouth never went away.

"Yes. Come upstairs for a chat? Hell, come up for a quickie."

When Tony reached for him, Cullen stepped back, raising his hands instinctively, which splashed him with hot liquid. "Ow! I mean, no. I mean, that's very sweet, but I have plans."

"Cullen? Everything okay?" Matt walked over, a slight frown marring his forehead.

"Yeah. Spilled some toddy, you know? Uh, this is Tony. Tony, Matt. Tony's an ad exec. He was on tour with us for a while." No babbling. He wasn't allowed to freak out over introducing an ex to a current lover, dammit. He was an adult.

"Matt Nathanson. Pleased to meet you. I hope your stay is going well?" Matt held one hand out, offering Tony a smile.

Tony shook Matt's hand, but the cool, calculating look in his eyes told Cullen something bad was brewing. So he took the bull by the horns. "Well, have a good one, dude. Matt and I are in for the night, you know?"

"You and…? Cullen, seriously?"

Cullen scowled, the urge to bump chests overwhelming his good sense. "Seriously what?"

Tony stepped closer, stage-whispering, "The staff? Not classy, Cee."

"Well, you just biffed that one, Tony." Cullen moved away. "Matt's so not the help, and he's also not a low-down cheater. I'm sure you'll find company. Night." He turned, begging Matt with his eyes not to say anything.

"Good evening, sir. If you'll excuse us." And just like that, Matt grabbed the tray and offered Cullen a tight smile.

Cullen followed quickly, hating that he'd come so close to making a scene in the lobby. That was a cardinal sin for a hotelier, and he knew it.

"You have a key close, or should I grab mine?" Matt asked.

"I have one." Cullen switched both cups to one hand. "I'm sorry, babe. He blindsided me."

"He's a stone-cold bastard, isn't he?"

"He is." Cullen fought with the key but managed to get the door open. "My management thought he would be a good look for me. That's awful, I know."

"Eh." Matt put the tray down and took the mugs from him to put them on the table.

Eh? Cullen had no idea what that meant. "I—that was a shitty thing to say. He wanted me to, well. He wanted to hook up, I guess, so he was pissed."

"Well, he's too late. I'm already here, and I don't intend to lose you. Sucks to be him."

Cullen stared a moment before a huge grin split his face nearly in half. "Promise?"

"You have my word."

Cullen grabbed Matt's upper arms and pulled him close, taking the deep, hard kiss he needed in order to show Matt how he felt. "Thank you."

"You're welcome. Come on, let's start a fire and put on easy-access pants. This asshole isn't worth stressing over. We have rum to drink."

"We do." He wrapped an arm around Matt's waist to steer him to the bedroom so they could change. "What did you order for supper?"

"I asked Dev to make us polenta and mushroom ragout like we talked about before. I thought we could share."

"Oh, that's the best part of Italy. You're amazing." Cullen loved this man. For real.

"I just… it's the best I can do."

"Hey." He pulled Matt to him, staring into those dark brown eyes. "It's perfect. I'm crazy about you, you know that?"

"I hoped so, yeah." Matt kissed him, almost chaste.

"Good." He hadn't used the L-word, so he wasn't allowed to be disappointed that Matt hadn't. "Okay, let's bathe. I want food."

"That's a good plan, honey." Matt kissed him again, soft and thorough. That move said a hell of a lot, giving Cullen hope for more soon.

He could make do with that for now. He really could.

## Chapter Twelve

**MATT** jogged down the stairs in the back of the hotel after checking that a loose stone on the back steps was fixed. He was making sure that maintenance was on point, and so far, so good.

He approved—the new maintenance guys were on the ball, and he hoped they'd stick around for the summer. That was always a gamble at resort areas. A lot of people headed downhill, where there was more rafting and hiking and all. Glenwood did huge business in the summer, and a lot of the workers went there before climbing back up out of the canyon for the snow.

The rock wall back here was crumbling a little. He knew it probably made no sense to try to shore it up until after the snows were gone, but they needed to put up some caution cones and some tape, maybe. That was a liability. He put that on his to-do list on his phone, took a picture, and kept going around the building.

The side gazebo had been well cleaned of snow, and the wet floor signs were clearly visible. The rose garden... well, now. It was smoking. Or rather, someone was smoking weed in it.

"Y'all do know that you can't smoke weed in a public area, don't you? It's sort of a thing, and we're a nonsmoking facility." He couldn't see the who, but he had a fairly good guess. "Not to mention that your coaches might bitch."

The guy who stepped out of the garden didn't have a joint with him, but he sure wasn't anyone Matt expected, either. "I don't have a coach, but I appreciate the sentiment."

*Ah, Cullen's ex. Goody.* "Well, this is considered public space, sir. I'm really sorry."

"Oh, no problem. We weren't sure what the hotel policy was."

A younger guy, one of the coaching assistants, slunk out of the garden and hustled away. Poor kid probably hadn't gotten what he wanted out of that.

Matt nodded and smiled. "Have a good day."

Obviously the ex wasn't waiting for Cullen. Thank goodness.

"Are you really dating Cullen?" the guy asked. Tony. His name was Tony.

*As if that's any of your business, fuckmonkey.* "We are in a relationship, yes." And if that was overreaching, then Cullen could let him know when he found out.

"Oh." Disappointment spread over Tony's face, and Matt felt a spurt of anger at the elaborate hurt Tony evinced. The guy had just been putting the moves on someone else.

"Well, I guess he has to settle for what he can get here."

"Indeed. It's a terrible hardship, to have to be in the most beautiful place on earth in the Treeline, but Cullen will persevere."

Tony's expression changed, hardening. "Oh, good. I don't have to be subtle. You know he's just dabbling with you, don't you? He's not as simple as he pretends to be."

Simple? His Cullen? Cullen worried things damn near as much as he did, and the man was a mass of hang-ups that Matt hadn't even started to understand, for fuck's sake. No, Cullen was like Chinese algebra. Hard to crack.

Matt shook his head wryly. "No wonder he broke up with you. You're an asshole. No smoking on the grounds or in the rooms. Just keep that in mind."

"Did you just call me an ass?"

"No, sir. I called you an asshole."

"I could have you fired."

"You could sure try." In fact, that would be funny as fuck, since it was legally impossible.

Tony clenched both hands into fists, and Matt wanted the guy to take a swing. Then again, that could just end badly for the hotel. "If you're contemplating assault, I need to tell you Colorado has some pretty strict laws on that, and I will press charges."

Not only that, he'd throw this motherfucker out of their hotel and make sure Tony hit the bottom of the main steps with a boot print on his ass.

His momma had taught him not to start it, but he'd be damned if he wouldn't finish it.

Three snowboarders came tumbling down the walk, jostling and laughing, stopping and appearing sheepish once they saw him. "Oh, hey! This is a great hotel. Right, Tony?"

Matt looked to Tony with a noncommittal smile, daring the snake to show his fangs.

"It's a lovely antique," Tony said with a sniff. "Later, guys."

"Dude, what crawled up his ass and died?" one of the men asked.

"Patrick." One of the guys shot him a grin made of pure naughtiness. "Patrick dumped him, hooked up with the pretty Texan here, and Tony's all butt-hurt. I fucking love it."

Matt's cheeks heated, but he had to laugh. Yeah, that about summed it up. "You guys need anything?"

"Is there something that we can order for snacks? So starved."

"There are complimentary snacks in the lobby, guys. Have at."

"Just pastries? We need protein."

"There's meat and cheese trays, and a thing of meatballs." Cullen had been more than clear about what athletes needed for fuel. More than. Dev had taken it to heart too. They had meat coming out their ears.

"Rock on!" They all high-fived.

"Enjoy, y'all." He waved, tugged his little watchman's cap down over his ears, and continued on his walk-through. He was so glad to see that most of Cullen's buddies weren't dicks. Mainly the ex….

A fairly recent ex too. Cullen hadn't said a word about the man, either. Was it because it was a sore spot? Because Tony had been evil? Because it was easy to just forget? What?

Matt hit the front steps, nodding at the valet. The porch was deserted, the rocking chairs clean, the steps salted. How much did he really know about Cullen beyond him being a prodigy with no real family left?

Well, he knew Cullen had a birthmark on his hip bone, right above where the golden curls started. He knew that Cullen slept on his right side, and that he brushed his teeth three times a day for exactly three minutes.

He also knew Cullen had a weakness for carbs, wanting pasta and garlic bread or carrot cake when he was super stressed. He knew Cullen's knees ached when the weather changed, knew where the man needed his Tens unit the most.

He bet that Tony asshole didn't know that. He'd bet the motherfucker didn't even care to know.

Matt drew in a deep breath, smiling at Carole, who was temping at the front desk. "Hey, lady. How goes it?"

"Excellent. We've got six rooms open for tonight, and I saw on Facebook that someone had tagged Mr. Patrick on the new pipes, so I bet we fill up. I know the restaurant's already booked."

"That's amazing." He nodded and smiled, but he was already making notes to check with Dev on servers and glassware. They kept losing glasses to the snowboarders, who kept them in their rooms for water and protein shakes.

"If you need someone at the desk permanently, Matt, I'm totally looking for a long-term position, just so you know, I mean."

"I'll check in with Belinda," he said, softening his words with another smile. "But I know she's praised your work."

"Cool. I know I'm young, but I want to work, and I love meeting all the people."

"You're doing great. Holler if you get too busy." Matt hustled for the kitchen to check in with Dev.

A hand reached down and grabbed him as he rushed through the closed dining room, Cullen's cold lips landing on his in a kiss that shattered his plans.

Matt gasped, then laughed, wrapping his arms around Cullen. "Hey."

"Hi! Where were you off to so fast?"

"To see Dev. How's your day been?"

"Good. I shredded some this morning, and I went over all sorts of shit with Yves. Reports on how energy efficient we are and all. We rock."

"Excellent. I want to watch you sometime. I've only seen videos." Another place they weren't in sync.

"You should come try. I know, I know, you're not wanting to fall down a lot, but it would be a hoot to spend some time together." Cullen's blue eyes lit up with enthusiasm, and it was hard to resist.

"Sure. I'd try. I mean, snow is soft." And he wanted to see what Cullen did, what the deal was. He wanted to know Cullen's... friends? Teammates? Fellow competitors?

"Well, kinda." Cullen laughed. "Still, we'll get you good snow pants."

"I have some." He loved his snowmobile, didn't he?

"Duh." Cullen rolled his eyes, then kissed Matt's nose. "So, you'll come up to the pipes while the guys are here?"

"Okay. Yeah. You promise they won't be evil? I'll be a good loser, but...." No one wanted to be made an ass of.

"They'll tease the hell out of you, but they love to teach people what we do." Cullen chuckled. "Hazing is mostly limited to the tour."

"Teasing is totally to be expected. I have frat brothers, remember." Heaven knew those bastards had pulled some shit on him and vice versa.

"Right. That seems so weird." Cullen rubbed their noses together. "I should let you go do your thing with Dev. Which sounds dirty."

"All those types of things are yours, Cullen." There. He'd said it.

"Good." The kiss he got left him blinking and breathless. Even more so when Cullen kinda groped him right there in the hall. "See you at lunch?"

"You know it. Uh, your ex? I sort of pissed him off a little."

"No shit?" Now a little evil glint crept into the blue of Cullen's gaze. "Tell."

"He was smoking green in the courtyard with some kid and threatened to have me fired when I called him an asshole." It had totally been worth it.

"Oh my God, you are so fucking amazing." Cullen hooted and danced him around in a circle.

"It felt good." He touched his lips to Cullen's. "He's a fucktard."

"He is." A grimace pulled at Cullen's mouth. "I thought he was perfect for me, you know? Undemanding. Didn't care that I was on the road all the time. Relatively charming at parties. I was an idiot."

Was Matt perfect? Suitable? Was asking just fishing?

"He never wanted to know me," Cullen said, hands on Matt's hips. "Not like you do. He never once strapped on a snowboard with me or took me on a wild snowmobile ride."

"I do. I mean, I was pissed as hell that you showed up, but… I'd be your friend even if we weren't more."

"I know. That means more to me than anything else." Cullen hugged him, just threw both arms around him and squeezed. "Love you, babe. Go get your work done." Cullen left in a whirlwind, just rushing out the door.

*Love you.*

Well, hell.

A slow smile bloomed across his face. "Love you too, Cullen."

The words disappeared in the empty dining room, but that was okay. He'd said them, he meant them, and that was what mattered.

He could say them in person later. Right now Dev needed to know they were expecting a full house.

## *Chapter Thirteen*

**TWO** feet of fresh powder overnight, a good grooming from the ground team, and Cullen was ready to get a hard workout in. Even better, Matt was supposed to meet him in an hour to get a lesson in. Cullen couldn't wait to get Matt on the starter loop.

He'd seen Matt on the sled. Matt could learn to do this, Cullen had no doubt. In fact, he kinda thought Matt would be good at it; he had good balance and a need for speed. He couldn't wait to show off what he could do.

He adjusted his helmet, walking his board to the edge of the pipe. Cullen took a deep breath, let half of it out, and tipped over the lip.

From there it was a matter of letting his body know what it was made for. Muscle memory was an amazing thing, from the first aerial to the last 720.

He landed solid, snow spraying. Fuck, yeah. That was what he needed.

"Sweet!" He heard Gianni shout from up top, and Cullen gave him a thumbs-up.

Cullen took the lift up this time, having hiked up to the ramp the first run to warm up his legs. The second run was better; then the third run felt wibbly-wobbly. Man, he was totally out of shape. He'd kinda… given up on the season, but he hadn't really told anyone yet.

He had a new life, a new reason. Matt made him feel as if he had a family, as if his life was whole. He'd been searching for that emotion so long.

"Patrick? Dude, your Texan is here. Tex, he's over here."

Tex? Oh, that was cute.

Cullen waved. "Hey! You stay there! I'll come to you." Matt needed training on the easy slope. No way was he going to put his lover on the big pipe.

That was a broken ankle waiting for a place to happen.

He hit the ramp again and kinda put on a show. No wobblies this time. Cullen pretended he was at the finals.

He swore he could feel Matt's eyes on him, watching him close. Cullen pushed it, because he had to just barge that last jump, really hope he didn't end up doing an asspass right by Matt.

The guys were hooting and hollering, just throwing a fit. Seriously, when he landed, Cullen pumped his arms as if he was getting a gold medal for his performance. Above the din he heard a hoot that was pure Southern male, and he grinned. Matt.

His stodgy lover was rednecking it up.

He unstrapped and shouldered his board once he got off the pipe, then hiked up to meet Matt. "Hey, babe!"

"Hey, you. That rocked. That was the prettiest thing I've seen in hours."

"Yeah?" His cheeks heated because they'd been… energetic this morning.

"Yes, sir." Matt grinned at him, and Cullen knew they were thinking about the same thing. "So, I'm gonna try this thing?"

"You are. I got you a board and boots. Let's get you geared up."

"I'm all yours. Try not to get me killed."

Cullen winked at Matt, then remembered he had his goggles on. He pushed them up so he could waggle his eyebrows. "You're way more valuable to me alive."

"Good to know."

He could see the hint of nerves in Matt's eyes.

"I told you how I feel." Cullen wanted Matt to know that was real. Like, really real.

"You did, love. Show me how to do this."

"You got it. Come on. We have a beginner slope, you know?" Cullen led the way, anticipation riding him hard.

"We might consider offering a package with lessons for adults. We're not really a family destination, but we could work something up."

"Oh, I know some guys who are amazing at teaching seniors." Cullen enjoyed the idea of integrating all their guests, helping bridge the generation gap.

"Yeah? It could happen."

He helped Matt clip into the board, staying close so his lover could find his balance. "It could. Okay, hold on to my hands and really get planted in your knees."

"Right. How old were you when you learned?"

"Maybe five?" Cullen grinned when Matt rolled his eyes. "I've taught fifty-year-olds. You have great balance. You can do this."

"I totally can."

That was what he loved best about Matt. His lover tried. No matter what life threw at the man, he tried. "So, now hold me and slide back and forth. Hinge at the hips and get a feel for the snow. It will be scratchy."

Matt frowned, and it took a second for him to get it, but he started moving, slow and easy.

Cullen walked Matt through a few flat snow maneuvers, then taught him how to stop. In a way it was great that Matt had never learned to ski, because the motions were so different and could foul people up.

Matt listened and went easy, laughing whenever he tumbled down. Cullen spent a bit of time on his ass too, because he was far more used to boarding than walking in the snow.

Different guys came and went—Joe hollering encouragement, Travis demonstrating how to turn. Before long, Matt was on the wee slope, doing a credible serpentine and blowing out some spray when he stopped.

"You're rocking it!" Cullen applauded, and Matt tried to bow, ending up face-planting, snow flying everywhere.

Cullen chuckled, going to help Matt up. "So are you sore yet?"

"My thighs are letting me know that they're not used to working so hard."

"I bet. You're doing amazing. Tell me when you're ready to quit. Or try your first trick." Cullen winked. He didn't want to sway Matt either way. He could hang out this way all day.

"I'm ready to try a trick?"

"I think so, yeah. I mean, you've learned to carve your turns, so maybe an ollie? That's like a jump off a bump here, like a speed bump that makes your car fly a little."

"I'll try. What's the worst thing that can happen?"

"Well, you could fall. Nice thing with an easy ollie is you're unlikely to break anything or really go tits up."

"Indeed." Matt rolled his eyes and he shot Cullen a grin. "Okay, what do I do?"

"I'll demonstrate." Cullen hustled over to strap back into his cups. "Okay, watch this time." He picked a gentle area of slope and cut back and forth, then went dead on for a moment to pick up speed, before hitting a bump with bent knees. He bounced up, pulling up with his legs to get some air.

Matt followed along, shaky and careful, too slow to make the trick, and down he went with a thump.

"You need more speed, babe, but I can tell you have the idea." Cullen was about to bust with pride. He'd taught teenagers with less bounce than his lover.

"Lemme try it again."

"Cool. The trick is to really dig in, then pull up in a frog position."

"Really dig in and then ribbit." Matt winked at him, just as playful as could be. That smile was brighter than the sun on the snow and a hell of a lot warmer.

Cullen demonstrated one more time, pushing off harder so Matt could see the simple trick in real time. "No pressure."

It took three more runs before Matt got it, but he managed it, popping up and landing on his board. Matt cheered along with the guys who were watching. Cullen heard a whoosh behind him, then some hotdogger zipped through without warning, clotheslining Matt and sending him flying down the hill on his back, arms and legs going every which way.

"Find out who that was," Cullen barked. "I want him escorted off the property." He kicked off downhill to get to Matt, his heart pounding. "Babe? Are you hurt?"

"I'm fine, I think." Matt sat up, blood on his face. "Just a little dazed and confused."

"Let me look." He eased off Matt's goggles, then his hat, looking for the source of the bleeding. There was a cut on Matt's eyebrow—not deep, but a bleeder. He grabbed a handful of snow and put it on Matt's forehead. "That'll stop it."

"C-cold." Matt smiled faintly. "Sorry. That was a—what do you call it? Wipeout in surfing."

"A beef. You didn't do it. That bizatch did it for you. When I find out who did it…," Cullen grumbled, unhooking Matt's board and getting him to his feet.

"Dude," Travis said, coasting up. "Everything solid?"

"I'm fine." Matt stood up on shaky legs. "I think it's time for me to head down to the Treeline and get cleaned up."

"Totally. I'll come with you." He didn't want to leave Matt alone, just in case he'd been hurt.

"You don't have to, love." Matt nodded, though.

There was no way he was going to let Matt go by himself. No way.

"I got you. You guys call me when you find the jerk," he told Travis.

"Will do, bud. We'll haul him down."

"Thanks." He put an arm around Matt's waist and pulled them off the course. "Do you want me to call for a cart?"

"No. No, I'm not hurt. I can do it. I can walk."

"Okay." Cullen had left their boards, but he'd bet Travis would deal with it. "Hold my hand at least?"

"I'd love to." Yeah, Matt's grip was a little shaky, a touch weak.

Cullen moved slowly, carefully. "Oh, love, you need a nice hot soak and some carb loading."

"I could soak, for sure. Soak and Tylenol."

"We'll get you all fixed up. You're a trouper, babe. I'm so sorry someone bum-rushed you that way."

"I'm sure it was an accident."

"I hope so." Cullen couldn't imagine what else it could be, but he knew panic had hit him hard when Matt went down. Like, total freak-out.

"I'm sure." Matt offered him a shaky grin. "I did okay, didn't I?"

"You did amazing." Cullen loved Matt even more for trying so hard. He just threw himself into everything with his full attention. They got down the hill, and thankfully, there was a shuttle waiting to take people back to the hotel. "Hey, Paul. Can we hijack you? Matt took a spill."

"Oh, dude. Sure. Come on. Hop in."

"Thanks." He shushed Matt when he would have protested. "That's a long way."

Matt leaned into him. "I guess no one's waiting for the shuttle right now."

"Nope. I don't see anyone." Cullen helped Matt up the stairs of the bus, wincing when he saw how stiff Matt already seemed. He wanted to get his lover naked, make sure all Matt's parts were intact.

Paul closed the doors and headed back down the hill. Cullen sat close to Matt, sharing warmth.

"I'm fine, Cullen. Just banged up. You've had tons worse, I bet."

"Probably, but you were out there because of me and I worry." Cullen chuckled. "I'm mother henning."

"You are. I'm cool. I was trying to get the hang of it. I'll have to go again soon. Maybe after the exhibition opening the pipes?"

"Totally. Things will slow down then, and we won't have to worry about asshats on the course." He was damned pissed about that. There was etiquette out there. There were fucking rules for a reason, and people not getting hurt was part of them.

Matt patted his leg. "See? You get to deal with this before we're really open."

"You know it. These are the things I usually just report to a manager." Cullen snorted. "I guess that's me right now. The things you don't think of."

"I know you have a good team. You'll find someone to take the reins."

The confidence Matt had in him humbled Cullen, made his chest swell up. He wanted to kiss Matt, but he knew that would push boundaries a little too far. He could wait.

"You're grinning very hard," Matt told him.

"I can't help it. You make me feel ten feet tall and bulletproof. The only thing that ever made me feel that way before was winning an event."

"Well, then, I must be doing something right."

"You definitely are." Cullen bounced to his feet when the shuttle stopped. "Come on, babe. Inside. We'll get hot tea and a bath."

Matt climbed off the bus, looking a little worse for wear. "Sounds like a plan, Mr. Patrick."

"Mr.—Nah. That was my dad. Maybe my grandpa, I guess. I forgot how everyone calls me Patrick. Is that weird? I haven't been off tour that long."

"Do you miss it?" Matt stomped the snow off his boots.

"Now that I have the pipes open here? Nah. The grind was getting to me." That was the truth too. He could board, teach if he wanted to, trade on his fifteen minutes of fame to make their park a success.

"It's a huge amount of pressure. All the sponsorships and stuff?"

"That and the travel. I had no idea how much I wanted to stay in one place." With someone to stay with. Yeah, Cullen loved that.

"Yeah? One day I want to travel, but right now I have this."

"Oh, dude. I want to take you to the Alps. You'll just be amazed." Cullen wanted to take Matt all over, but he didn't want to run from resort to resort all year.

"One day, maybe. Right now we have a lot to do."

Wow, he loved how Matt talked about them in the long term. They hadn't sat down and discussed it or anything, but Cullen felt as though they were settled, like they were going to be together-together.

Assuming someone didn't kill Matt on the runs, of course.

Cullen scowled. Yeah, he needed to nip that in the bud. He looped an arm through Matt's to help him down from the bus.

"Matt? Are you okay?" Belinda headed down the stairs. "They called from the slopes. Are you all right?"

"I'm fine." Matt spread his hands. "No one needs to make a fuss. I just had a fall, is all."

"Oh, good. They made it sound scary."

"No. Not at all."

"He went down pretty hard. Could you get the kitchen to send up a tray? Nibbles and tea?" Cullen had to admit he loved room service at home. He was such a dork.

"Absolutely. I'm totally on it. You two get upstairs before someone else needs something, why don't you?"

Cullen nodded and hustled Matt to the elevator. "Hot water."

"Yes, boss." Matt actually kissed his nose. In public.

Cullen beamed. Okay, so maybe he owed the board bomber a tiny bit of gratitude. Matt was kinda goofy when he was shook-up. Goofy Matt was adorable.

They boarded the elevator, and Matt leaned against him. "Man, how do you wipe out like that and go do another run?"

"It's my job." It had been, anyway. Now he wasn't sure.

"I didn't realize how tough it was. You all make it look so easy to just pop up."

Cullen snorted. "Sometimes it is. I tore my quad once. They hauled me away yelling my head off."

"Oh Jesus. I guess so." Matt shook his head, squeezed him. "My stud."

That made his cheeks heat, and Cullen felt ridiculously pleased. He kissed the corner of Matt's mouth "Yep. So yours."

Matt nodded, and Cullen headed them toward his apartment. His rooms were bigger, more comfortable, and had the whirlpool tub. They really just needed to move Matt's bed to his place. He'd cleaned out a lot, packed away the stuff he and/or Matt wanted to keep of Grandpa's, and gotten new floors put in.

It was starting to feel like home.

"You ought to move your bed in, you know? Free up a suite?"

Matt looked over at him. "You think so?"

"I do. I also have a whole wall I can free up for built-ins for your books and movies." Cullen felt super brave just asking.

He felt Matt's hand, fingers squeezing his butt. "I could handle that."

"Most excellent." Man, his heart was pounding as if he'd just done a backside 540.

"Yeah. Yeah, I think it is." Matt turned toward him, kissed him nice and easy.

Cullen laughed with sheer joy, but he kept his hug gentle. No squeezing Matt's bruises.

"Come bubble with me, love." Matt tugged him to the bath.

Love.

*That's right.*

He loved Matt more than anyone he'd ever known. What a damned good day.

## *Chapter Fourteen*

**MATT** woke up so sore he might just die. He couldn't let anyone know, because that would just upset Cullen, but there wasn't an inch of him that didn't ache. He looked down at his body, which was bare because he'd kicked off the sheets. Oh, hello Technicolor. That was impressive and a little bit like he'd wrecked on his motorcycle. There was no road rash, but the rest looked pretty much the same.

He reached for Cullen, then frowned. Oh, right. They had the big ribbon cutting—well, sometime. Tonight, maybe? *Get up. Up. Up. Moving. Dressing. Working.*

His phone beeped, and Matt hunted for it, surprised to find it neatly plugged in on Cullen's charging station. Good man.

He grabbed it, hitting his e-mail to check. Seven hundred e-mails?

*What the hell?* Matt scowled, flipping one open even as he got up and headed to the bathroom.

*Dude. Wipeout!*

The next one read, *Real professional there.*

What the hell?

Every one he opened had either a high five from some snow bunny or a snarky comment about his lack of professionalism. Matt had no idea how all these people had gotten his e-mail.

Finally, one of the e-mails pointed to a YouTube video, and he went to look, surprised as hell to find a title screaming, "Hotel Manager Tries to Fly in Epic Wipeout."

The little blurb underneath said, "Who else thinks this blazing raisin should stick to old folks' hotels?"

He hit the Play button because he had to. You couldn't do damage control without knowing the whole situation.

There was a three-minute video of him busting his ass, over and over, goofy ragtime music playing in the background, and the final shot was him wiping out at the end and sitting up, blood freezing on his face. Then there was a graphic that just said, "Loser" and his e-mail address.

He sighed. Dammit. This was so not what the grand opening of the winter park needed. First he needed to get that video off YouTube. Then he'd move on. He messaged the person who loaded the video, put a privacy violation up, and then flagged it, knowing that no one would do a damn thing. Then he called Yvonne to see what her marketing advice might be.

"Matt. You have a secret admirer."

"You think?"

"How's your head?" she asked.

He sighed and pulled on his socks. "Better than my legs."

"Ouch. Well, it looked painful. I reported it for TOS violation."

"Yeah. You think I need to do anything?"

"I don't think so. Surely it'll be gone by noon if we're lucky."

Matt slipped into his shoes. "I sure hope so. I mean, it's more humiliating than anything, but we certainly don't need bad press right now. I need to check on the ribbon-cutting stuff. Let me know if I need to be making a statement."

"A statement saying what? You're willing to learn to snowboard? You're willing to try new things? Who's going to fuss?"

"The historical society," Matt said, rolling his eyes.

"Bah. Yves followed all the rules when he designed the park. They can't complain about anything real."

"Right. I'll just own it. Is that what you're telling me?"

"Yep." Yvonne snort-laughed happily. "Hold your head up, grin, and say, 'Why yes, that was me.'"

"Yeah, you should see the bruises on my face. There's no question. I'll be down in a few."

"Don't be surprised if you get a standing O."

"Oh for f…." He hung up and grabbed his tie and his sport coat. Dev would have to help him put it on.

Should he text Cullen? Matt wasn't sure because Cullen would be out making sure everything was ready for the ribbon cutting. Eh, Cullen would just threaten to kill someone, and he wanted to be closer for that.

The thought buoyed Matt, making him grin.

"Dude, that was an epic crash. You're legit." One of the snowboarders stopped him on the way down the stairs, which he was navigating slowly. "You can shred with me anytime."

"Thank you. I'm going to figure this out, you just wait and see."

"I have faith." The guy high-fived him before trotting off. Whoever had tried to make Matt look so bad might just have outsmarted himself.

He wasn't a robot, for fuck's sake, and he wasn't seventy years old, either. Matt had looked up "blazing raisin," which implied he was really old. Fuck that. If Cullen had taught him anything, it was that stodgy didn't work for him.

Or it didn't have to. Either way, what bliss.

He made it into the lobby, where a news van was pulling up. *Lord, let them be here about Cullen and not me.*

Geoff ran up the stairs, all panicky face. "Boss. What do I do?"

Matt chuckled. "Find out who they need to talk to, and we'll get them set up."

"Okay. Okay, yeah. Your face is... dude. You face-planted hard."

"You think?"

Geoff flushed. "Sorry, boss. I mean, one of the guys told me how someone cut you off and all. That sucks."

"Hey, I'm new to this. Face-planting is part of the process." Oh, that sounded so... meta.

"Yeah, better you than me. Not a snow bunny." Geoff grinned and headed off the news team by running back down the steps and pulling out valet tickets.

Right. Time to run.

**"YVES,** you have that speech ready?" The ribbon cutting was, maybe, two hours away, and Cullen had too much shit to do. Hell, he hadn't even been able to text Matt today, and he wanted to touch base, see if Matt was pissed about the YouTube thing.

At least a hundred people had sent it to Cullen.

Fucker. He knew this had to be Tony. Had to be. Still, Matt hadn't thrown a fit as far as he could tell, and, fuck, talk about try. All of the e-mails Cullen had gotten were positive. About how he'd made a good choice in managers.

Shit, his grandpa had made a good choice. Cullen was just smart enough to keep him.

"Mr. Patrick, can you sign this? It's a release for me to give the news guys a tour of the park."

"Sure. Absolutely. Be careful. Are you taking the shuttle up?"

"We are." The kid grinned. Ty. That was his name. One of Cullen's first hires, and he thought the guy would do great.

"Excellent. You know how to find me." Dude, he sounded like Matt. Then again, Matt was a good teacher.

"Okay, Cullen, I have my speech." Yves popped up next to him looking so nervous.

"It's a five-minute thing. Just don't lapse into French or German."

"*Oui.*" Yves winked at him, face wrinkling. "Your friend, he was very determined out there, yes?"

"Matt?" Cullen chuckled. "He's my lover, Yves. He knows how important this is to me, so he wants to share it."

"You are lucky there. That shows of a good man."

"It does." Cullen gave Yves a man hug. "Thanks for everything."

"Are you pulling on my leg? This is my gateway to American work."

"Well, if you need me to talk to any clients, just let me know. I'll be happy to."

"I will use you as a reference." Yves beamed. "Go and check all your things. I'll be fine."

What he wanted to do was to check on Matt.

Cullen stepped off to one side of the office above the pipes and pulled out his phone. He texted, not wanting to interrupt if Matt was with a guest.

As he was texting, his phone rang, and it was the Treeline's front desk. Cullen blinked, then hit the green button. "Patrick."

"Cullen, you've got a group of people here saying that they're your guests?"

"Yeah?" He frowned, going over the event schedule in his mind. "Not the newsies?"

"Nope. These are not media folks, I don't think."

"Okay, it will take me ten minutes or so to get down there. Can you get them a coffee and a snack?" He had no idea who was there, but Dev would make them happy while they waited.

"Of course. I'll let them know."

Guests. Him. Huh.

He hopped into his little golf cart once he got downstairs. The grounds guys had worked their asses off to clear the walkways and roads, so he coasted right down to the hotel. They were expected to get another huge dump overnight, but by then all the media should be gone. Then he could just have fun on the pipes and the round and—Yeah, he wanted to ride. He wanted to get Matt back up there too, just the two of them. They would have a ball, and Matt would get to see what speed was like on a board instead of a sled.

And there would be no clotheslining and sending Matt flying, dammit.

He pulled up in front of the hotel and handed off the cart. He sure hoped his guests didn't mind snow pants. Of course, Belinda said these guys weren't media. He'd bet they were boarders.

When he saw the little group in the VIP area, Cullen stopped dead and stared a few moments. His sports agent. His coach. His publicist. *What the fuck?* He'd invited all of them, sure, but everyone had turned him down.

"Hey, guys, you came!" He hoped his shock sounded more happy and excited.

"We did." Dan Myers, who'd been his coach since his teens, broke from the group and came to give him a hug. "How's it going?"

"It's going. The pipes are crunchy. I can't wait to show you." Maybe Dan could try new kids up here.

"I'm glad." Dan leaned close. "Steve and Paul are here because Tony says you're retiring. Is that true?"

He felt the corners of his eyes pull wide and his cheeks heat. "Tony did what?"

"He called Steve." Steve was the publicist, the one who would sound the alarm. "Steve panicked and called us. Now, I told him I knew you were thinking about it, but you hadn't let me know. You would tell me before you announced."

"Of course I would." He smiled tensely at Steve and Dan. "I mean, I've got a grand opening today. I wasn't planning on any announcements."

"You're going to leave all the life for an old hotel, Cullen? Seriously? This isn't you." Steve looked utterly horrified.

"How do you know?" He wanted to clap his hand over his mouth, but it was out there now. "Look, I want to give you guys the tour and all, but I have a billion details to deal with. Can you wait about half an hour?"

"Sure. Uh. Tony said there were rooms available?"

"Yes. I'm sure there are." Even if he had to go clean a room himself. And kick Tony out. "Let me check in with Belinda. Did you get some snacks?"

"I have a lovely selection of finger sandwiches here, and some pastries. The coffee service will be out shortly." Matt surprised them, standing there like an avenging angel, a superhero, a bruised Texan, whatever. "You'll need three VIP rooms, yes? I've got y'all taken care of. The rooms need another half an hour, but we can hold your bags, if you need."

Thank God. Cullen's panic popped, a disappearing bubble, and he beamed at Matt. "Dan this is Matt Nathanson, the manager here at the Treeline. Matt, Dan Myers. My coach."

"I've heard so much about you, Mr. Myers. Welcome to the Treeline."

"Thanks." Dan shook hands. "Come meet the rest of Cullen's dream team."

"I'd be honored." Matt shot him a warm, happy look.

Cullen swallowed his heart, which had jumped into his throat, and grinned back. "I'll be back for that tour, okay?"

"I'll take care of your guests, Cullen. Trust me."

"I do." He wanted to kiss Matt as much as he wanted to kick Tony's ass. Maybe more. Yeah, no. Tony was being a fuckmonkey. Time to go put a stop to that right now. He could waste maybe five minutes on it. He didn't want Tony here. He didn't want the son of a bitch messing with the ribbon cutting or interfering with him spending the evening taking care of his lover, who was plastered all over social media.

It was bad enough that he was going to have to talk to his team about rejoining the tour, or not, before he was ready to make that call. But messing with his fucking hotel? Oh, no.

He headed upstairs, and he didn't bother to knock on Tony's door. He just used his master key.

"Aren't you supposed to knock first, lover? I'm glad you decided to come visit." Tony was in a robe, sprawled out in a chair by the window.

"Are you? Are you still gonna be glad when I kick your ass out?"

"Now, now. Don't be bitchy. What are you all caught up about?"

"You called Steve? Hell, you called in my whole team! You had no right to do that." He stomped over, staring at the face he used to find so attractive.

"You need to remember what you're made for. You're not a hotelier."

"No, but I own a hotel. My family has owned this place for years. I like it here, and I worked my ass off to build that winter park and make it work with this place. What do you want me to do? Go back on tour and pretend that you're not fucking every intern that comes along?" Cullen was shaking, he was so pissed off.

"Come back on tour. I made a mistake, lover." Tony opened his robe, exposing that perfectly manscaped body. "Come back to me."

"I told you, Tony. I'm with Matt now." He wasn't even the least bit tempted by the perfect gym muscles or gleaming spray tan.

"You do realize you're slumming, don't you?"

Seriously? He was a fucking boarder. Where the hell did they slum? "No, I realize how fucking lucky I am. I want you out before the ceremony." He would carry Tony out tied to a luggage cart if he had to.

"You're not serious." Tony closed his robe, eyebrows drawing together.

"You could have really hurt him with your stunt— not embarrassed him, not hurt the hotel. Hurt Matt. He gives a shit about me, Tony. He's into me because I'm me, nothing else."

"You really think so?" Tony stood, pacing to the decanter that sat on the business desk in his suite. "I looked into him. He has an ironclad contract. Why not make it more appealing by fucking the owner?"

If only Tony knew that Cullen had done the pursuing, he'd chased Matt and seduced him. He'd been the one who asked Matt to move in. And every time they were together, Matt gave Cullen that happy, wondering look and nodded like this was magic.

His anger backed down just as his panic had earlier. He didn't owe Tony any explanations. The guy was a douche who'd cheated on him and left him in the middle of a rough season when his dad was so sick.

"Fuck off, Tony. I mean it. Out. You're banned from the hotel for endangering the staff."

"You're making a huge mistake, Cullen. I'm an advertising expert. I can ruin this place." Tony drew up to full height, looking down at him.

"No. You can't. Because it's made of awesome. This place is sweet." He raised his voice at the end of the last word in a boarder habit that he knew Tony hated. "I'll send a bellman for your bags in twenty."

"You fucking prick. I'll destroy you."

"Yeah, I don't think so, mister. Go find someone else to screw with." Cullen turned on his heel, his skin prickling while he waited for Tony to go all primal and try to hit him with a bottle or something. It didn't happen, and he grabbed his cell on the way down the hall so he could call the bell desk. He needed to warn the front desk, and Matt too. Maybe Dan.

God.

"Treeline Bell desk."

"Hey, James, 304 is checking out. Can you send a cart?"

"You got it. It'll be ten, give or take. We're getting a rush of check-ins."

"Thanks."

He hung up and called Matt.

"Hey, stranger. Did you see that I'm an Internet sensation?"

"I did. I mean, a bazillion people did, but that'll be great for the new park." Cullen had this urge to just run and hide, but Matt sounded calm. Amused.

"Uh-huh. For the most part, people have seen the face and been kind."

"You did bruise up. I didn't want to wake you before I left."

"I appreciate the sleep. Did you have lunch?"

"No. I don't think I have time, babe. I have to talk to my team. Tony called them in, told them I was going to announce my retirement today. They're all in a panic." He was feeling kinda hunted.

"Did he now? Well, don't let anybody push you into anything you don't want to do. You just make your own mind up."

Christ, he loved this man. "I—Can we meet in the kitchen? Just for a minute? I need a bite, and I need to see your face."

"Surely. Give me five, and I'll be there."

He heard a voice saying, "Matt? Matt, can you look at this, please?"

"Give me eight. See you in a few." *Click.*

Cullen snorted. Yeah, some things never changed. The bellman passed him on his way to the kitchen, and he grinned. The idea of kicking Tony out made him happy. Deeply.

Dev and the new guy were working their asses off, old-school hip-hop competing with the clink and clang of the pots and pans. The whole kitchen smelled of red sauce.

"It smells good in here," Cullen said.

"We're full enough that I thought an Italian menu would be easy and keep costs down so we could focus on the ribbon cutting. Matt hired out the sweet stuff, thank goodness. You need something? Matt hasn't come for his bagel or his coffee yet."

"Just a bite. I can make us something. Matt will be here in a mo." His belly rumbled, and Cullen was glad Matt had mentioned food.

"There are sandwiches in the staff fridge—ham, turkey, and tuna fish."

"That rocks." He gave Dev a one-armed hug as the guy passed. "Have I said thank you for everything you do, Dev?"

"Every time I get a paycheck." He got a wink and a wicked grin.

"Well, there is that." Cullen let Dev get back to work, going to the big fridge and pulling out sandwiches and Cokes before grabbing a couple of bags of chips from a basket on the counter.

"Can you tell Matt I'm in the storeroom? I just want five minutes of quiet."

"Of course. You just go breathe."

"Thanks." Cullen took lunch to the storeroom, settling on a stool. Okay. Breathing.

It took a few minutes, then the door opened, and Matt poked his head in. "Cullen?"

"Right here."

"Good deal." Matt looked a little like Frankenstein's monster, with the bruising and the cuts.

Cullen winced. "Oh, babe. You look as if you've been through the war. I got one of each sandwich."

"I'm good. Rumor is the owner threw someone out of the hotel. I would've paid to be a fly on that wall."

Cullen snorted. "Well, it sounds more dramatic than it was. He was all naked and trying to seduce me, so I guess it would have been interesting to eavesdrop."

"Obviously that didn't work."

"Nope." Cullen got up and went to wrap his arms around Matt. "Man, can we call today off?"

"Nope. Everyone is ready for the ribbon cutting." Matt held him, though, so easy. "What part's freaking you out?"

"That I want to retire." There. He'd said it.

"Yeah, that's a big deal."

Sometimes he wanted his Texan to lose his cool, melt down a little bit. Maybe wring his hands. "Yeah. I mean, I was going to break it to the guys gently, but they're all here expecting an announcement."

"So don't announce if you don't want to. Is that a thing? I mean, if you don't, what happens?"

"I don't want to deal with this logically, Matt."

"Oh. Right. Fucking asshole prick Tony, screwing with your timeline. I'll go put a boot in his ass."

"Thanks." He bobbed his head. "Except he's leaving."

"We aren't being logical, love. Shit, fuck, butthead. Let the beatings commence!"

"Right! We'll cut his ass." Cullen couldn't stop laughing now, his belly aching with it.

"We'll stomp a mud smear of the little fuck and walk it dry!"

"Oh. So Texas." He hooted and clung to Matt, wheezing. "I do love you."

"Good." Matt kissed him, good and hard, and that shut him up, that laser focus all on him.

Cullen paused to breathe, then kissed Matt right back. "Okay. I need to eat so I can go tell my guys how much I suck. They'll blame it all on Tony, which is nice."

"Let's eat, then. I'm all over that. Do you want me up at the ribbon cutting or down here dealing with this end of things?" Matt plopped down on a box and grabbed his sandwich.

"If you can come up, I would love you to be at the ribbon cutting." Cullen grabbed a tuna sandwich.

"I'll be there. All the transportation is set up and ready to go?"

"Yeah. The guys did great, and Brandon is here with his car in case anyone has mobility issues."

"Good. I want all the people down off the hill before nine, no question. That storm should be here around midnight, and I want everyone safe."

"Shit, I forgot about weather. Is it gonna ice? I thought it was just pow pow." Cullen fought the urge to grab his phone and check, because Matt had his back and would know anything he needed to know. This might be their only time all day together.

"It's supposed to be icy on the front end. No worries, we're just very booked. Tomorrow it'll be a winter wonderland."

"Sweet." Would he have time to brush his teeth? Tuna was a strong thing.

"You know that I have your back, no matter what you decide to do about your career, okay? The Treeline is yours, and it will always be your home."

"I know." He did. Cullen felt settled in his brain and his heart. He just wanted to get the hard part over. He knew his publicist would scream, and he'd have to do something legal about his contract with his agent. Dan was going to be really bummed, but he had a host of other boarders he could take on and a whole new place to train.

"Good deal. That's the important part."

"Thank you, Matt. You have no idea how good it feels to have someplace to come home to."

Matt grinned at him. "Hey, I hear you. For a little bit there, I thought I'd lost my someplace. I lucked out."

"I would turn the whole thing over to you before I would take it away." He meant it too.

"Well, if I'm right, you and I intend to head the same way, together, so it's not on the table for shit to worry about."

"Nope. We move your bed into my place. Paint the walls something soothing…." He winked. "Okay, babe, I have to go give the tour so I can change clothes and get everything together for the news guys." He'd put it off long enough.

"Take care of yourself. I have everything under control down here." Matt winked, then rolled his eyes. Yeah, Cullen got that. Nothing in the hotel business was really under control.

"See you in a bit." He bent to kiss Matt's lips, hoping his lover could forgive the tuna. Okay, he could do this.

He didn't have a choice. He had a whole new life to get on with.

**MATT** swung up into the shuttle, knowing he was running short on time to get up the hill. He'd make an appearance at the ribbon cutting, make sure Cullen saw him, and then—

"Hold up." He stopped dead and met the gaze of a certain unwanted advertising guy. "Get off the shuttle."

"This is a public event." Tony stood up, and Matt felt every inch of his bruised body tense up but refused to let it show.

"Not that public. Get off the shuttle."

"Make me." Tony sneered, standing at least three inches taller than Matt and really trying to work it to his advantage.

"Seriously?" As if he was going to risk an assault charge and miss the ceremony. He grabbed his walkie-talkie. "Security to the shuttle, please. We have a situation."

"Sad." Tony made a dramatic gesture. "Cullen deserves someone who will fight for him."

"Uh-huh. Like you were fighting off that kid in the rose garden the other night? You're lucky I didn't press charges against the guy you got to buzz me at the park." He had a future to worry about and fifteen guests watching with wide eyes. "Please exit the shuttle and the premises. You are not welcome at the Treeline for endangering our guests."

See him. See him not pop the bastard on the nose.

Tony opened his mouth, but security showed up, two sturdy men he'd not really met. They knew who he was, clearly, so he waved a hand at Tony. "This gentleman is just leaving, guys. Please make sure he makes it off the premises." Then he met Tony's gaze. "I will contact the authorities if you return, sir."

"You belong together," Tony snarled. "A has-been and a never-was." The guy stomped off, followed by two grinning security guards.

"Pardon the interruption, y'all. Shall we get this show on the road?"

"Yes, sir." The driver waited for Matt to take a seat, then shut the doors and eased them off toward the winter park, which was lit up like Christmas. Still, until you topped the rise just behind the hotel, it wasn't obvious and didn't hurt the view at all. In fact, the whole thing had cost more than he'd wanted, but it had been worth it, he thought. The hotel needed new blood, fresh energy.

And Cullen. He was tireless, working with the designer Yves to keep everything Colorado, ecofriendly, and in keeping with the Treeline.

"Mr. Matt?" The young girl leaning over the top of the seat smiled at him, one of her front teeth missing. "Is Cullen Patrick and Mookie Barber going to be there at the top of the pipe?"

"Cullen is definitely going to be there. I know he has a bunch of his buddies from the tour ready to sign autographs." Mookie? What the hell was a Mookie?

"Cool. I want to shred when I get bigger."

"Good for you!" He beamed at her because that was part of his job now, wasn't it? Encourage guests to snowboard.

And not face-plant like him.

Did Cullen have a waiver for people to fill out? Surely he did. Cullen was, if nothing else, acutely aware of the legal liabilities of his sport.

Matt had to wonder how the meeting with Cullen's team had gone. They hadn't talked since. What if they'd talked Cullen into one more season? If they had, it would suck a little—mainly because he was used to having Cullen's support, not just around the hotel, but emotionally, having a partner, a real friend, and lover. Something to love beyond the Treeline.

Still, where was he gonna go? He'd wait here for Cullen if he had to. They were a matched set.

Him. Cullen. The Treeline.

Warmth bloomed in his belly. No, Cullen didn't want to leave. He knew it, and he would bet his job that Cullen was going to retire. Maybe not publicly today, but soon.

One way or the other, Cullen was home, finally.

They got to the lot at the park, and Matt helped make sure everyone got where they were going before heading up to the office. Hopefully he could catch Cullen there. He was running too late. The crowd was already built up at the ribbon, and he beat feet to get close enough that Cullen would know he was there.

No matter what Cullen said, Matt wanted Cullen to see him, to feel his support.

He made it to the front of the crowd, seeing Cullen standing there with Yves and some of Ski Aspen's big names. Cullen's coach, Dan, was there, along with a couple of snowboarders Matt recognized.

Cullen searched the crowd, those blue eyes hunting, and Matt knew who he was looking for. He waved and moved toward the barriers, moving slow as he slogged through snow and fans.

A smile broke out on Cullen's face, and he waved, which made the crowd part to let him up. Cullen met him halfway, hand under his elbow to help him up to the platform at the top of the pipes.

"Hey there. I had to get rid of a couple of problems, but I made it."

"You did, and just in time. We're about to fire up the mic."

Cullen's coach held out a hand to shake. "You're a lucky guy, getting all of this one's energy."

"I am. Very." Matt didn't even have to think. This was his dream. He hadn't known it, because when Ben died, all Matt could think about was the hotel, about taking it back to its glory days. Now he knew it was about family. Theirs.

Cullen looked so proud he might explode. "Okay, ready for the sound, guys."

"Knock 'em dead, love."

Cullen reached over and squeezed his hand, then stepped up and grabbed the microphone. "Thank you all so much for coming to the grand opening of the Treeline Winter Park and Arena!"

The crowd applauded, and Matt tuned out a little, watching the faces, gauging reactions. His manager mind was also pondering how much hot chocolate they needed, and he made a note to text Dev while Yves did his speech.

Hot chocolate and more of those s'more desserts that Dev was planning. This was a big crowd, and they were going to be colder than anyone had anticipated.

Yves droned on for a few extra moments. Cullen took back the mic. "In a few moments, we're going to have an exhibition from my friends Mookie Barber and Jean Merida. I can't wait for you to see these pipes in action, but I have an announcement to make."

Matt caught his breath, turning to stare at Cullen, waiting.

"I've decided to retire from professional snowboarding to stay here at the Treeline and run my winter park while my partner, Matt Nathanson, runs the hotel my family worked so hard to build. I'm really excited about this new chapter in my life, and I'm so excited to see what the future holds for me and Matt, who is my partner in life, as well. Take it away, guys!"

A roar sounded from the crowd, and lights flashed wildly, but Matt only saw one man, his one man.

He took the one step that separated him from Cullen and pushed into his lover's arms, just like some crazy gay movie. Cullen kissed him until his ears rang, his lips warming right up.

The roar seemed to get louder, but that may have just been his heartbeat in his ears. He didn't care. Cullen was staying with him, and they were going to do this thing.

He had no idea if guardian angels were a thing, but maybe he had one. Maybe Ben had done this for them.

## Chapter Fifteen

**CULLEN** felt sore, and his face hurt a little from smiling so much. The ribbon cutting had flown by, the meal afterward so busy he hadn't had time to pee or breathe. By the time he dragged his ass upstairs, Matt had texted and told him he would be up in fifteen. He was just gonna snag Italian cream cake from the kitchen.

Cullen staggered into his apartment, and when he plowed into the bedroom, he almost killed himself on the edge of the bed, which was totally out of place.

Because it wasn't his bed. It was Matt's.

*Oh. Oh, fuck yeah.* He didn't care how much his cheeks ached, he had to smile. Somehow Matt had made this happen, today of all days. The bedroom was so clean it squeaked, all his laundry done and folded neatly in the little paper wrappers that meant they'd been sent out. He heard the soft knock before Matt used his key.

"You here already? I brought some snacks."

"I was just heading in so I could pee." Cullen ran to the bathroom because he didn't want any interruptions. "I think the day went well."

He could hear rattling and then the soft grunt as Matt plopped down on his sofa.

"I do too." Cullen finished up and scrubbed his hands. He hurried back out to the main room, sliding in at the couch like a runner sliding into third base. "Hi."

"Hey, my retired life partner." Matt tugged off his tie, turning from General Manager Extraordinaire to easygoing Texan.

"Hey, babe. You enjoyed that part, I guess?" Things needed to be perfectly clear, and Cullen had thought that was the best way.

"That most definitely did not suck." That grin lit the whole universe up.

Cullen laughed, clapping his hands with pure joy. "So, what did you bring?"

"Dev called it his honeymoon package for men. So beer, chips and queso, and tacos."

"Cream cake?" They'd had Italian earlier, and Cullen had missed dessert.

"I didn't forget."

"You're a rock star." Chuckling, Cullen jerked his chin toward the bedroom. "We could mess up the bed."

"We could. You like how it fits?"

"I do. It's going to be amazing." Rising, he started flinging off clothes. They didn't have to get busy; Matt was still all bruised, and they were both pooped. He just wanted to get comfy and snuggled.

"Good deal." Matt stripped off and grabbed the tray. "Get in bed, love, so I can hand this over."

"Yep!" The bedroom seemed so far away, and Cullen leaped for the bed from the doorway.

Matt was laughing as the tray was offered over. "Giant dork. Does retiring mean we can eat pasta whenever we want now?"

"Uh. No." Not yet. Not until he'd done all the appearances his publicist had scheduled for him. Steve had been pretty calm, really, saying it was easier to schedule him when he wasn't competing, and they could get at least a year out of his retirement announcement.

"Damn." Matt winked at him. "I think I deserve queso for working all day."

"We deserve anything we want tonight. Seriously." The tray balanced on the bed just fine, so Cullen dipped a chip and fed it to Matt. "How's the face?"

"Ugly, but Tylenol is all I need." Matt looked out the huge windows that faced the mountains. "Looks like your snow is here."

"Yeah?" Big fat flakes fell out there, some of them splatting on the glass. "That's, like, the perfect end to the best day."

"You settled in your head, love?"

He hadn't thought he'd ever be really settled, not really. Now he had this whole new family, friends, a home with history.

He had a partner too.

"I am. I mean, I never imagined any of this, but I love my life."

"I guess Ben knew what he was doing." Matt popped one of the beers open and offered it over.

"I think he must have." Gratitude flooded him. Cullen had no idea what the old guy had been thinking, but yeah. He was so deep in love he could only think someone had guided Grandpa Patrick's hand.

"Come on, love. Pick something on the tube. Rumor is that I have some time to sleep in tomorrow morning."

"No shit?" Now that was more precious than gold. Cullen grabbed the remote, the smell of queso and warm chips almost as comforting as the feel of Matt snuggling up next to him.

"No shit. I love you, Mr. Patrick."

"I love you too, you stodgy old manager." He kissed the corner of Matt's mouth. "How about *Top Chef* reruns on Hulu?"

"Mmm. The season with Richard Blais and Fabio. I like the bromance."

He grinned. Right, stodgy. His goofy, amazing lover.

It wouldn't be the last time Matt proved him wrong.

**"MATT?** Matt, that hiking group? The ones that wanted to go white-water rafting? They're very unhappy with the weather...."

"Get hold of that trampoline park, see if they have an opening for a party of twenty. They need the business, and those teenagers need a way to burn off energy." He shot Belinda a smile on his phone as he skipped down the back stairs. He had to get some paperwork done and sign off on the information for the high school senior prom, which was being held here in three weeks. One hundred percent occupancy for four days. Hot damn. Parents and teachers alike were all over the kids not having to drive, and Dev was in heaven with all the weird finger foods his staff got to make.

"Matt? Cullen is up in the new executive suite. He needs your input."

"Tell him I'll be there in three." He turned on the bottom step and headed back up from basement to the second floor. His old apartment renovation was almost finished, Cullen taking the reins and turning it into a high-tech business suite. Apparently TV people and biggie wow coaches needed 24-7 access.

Worked for him, because that meant a good economic reason to put in T-1 lines. Hooray, high-speed Internet.

He slowed before he hit the door to the public hall, face calm and cool.

"Mr. Nathanson! Amazing renovation on the mountain-view rooms." One of their older clients came by, golf shirt and pants pressed and clean. "Off for a game."

"Excellent. Good game, Mr. Harris." He used his master key to open the door to the executive suite. "Cullen? You needed me?"

"Hey, babe! Come give this a look for me." Cullen waved him into the room. "Smart TV is set up in the main room here, but do you think the TV that sinks into the cupboard is too much for the bedroom?"

"If you have a bunch of athletes in here, you'll have to have one that disappears somehow," he teased. Assessing how to have snowboarders and mountain cyclists and other athletes as their guests was a learning curve and a half. They'd lost more towel bars in the last six months....

"I think you're right." Cullen chuckled. "Nev wants to know if the tile in the bathroom is soothing enough."

Their designer, Neville, was dancing the dance of the historical versus the modern. He was cheating a little with this suite, but since it had been a private apartment, last decorated in the sixties, no one could bitch.

"Soothing? What does that even mean? I want to know that it looks clean."

"It's very river rock, babe." Cullen's blue eyes twinkled, and he nodded toward the bath.

"It's… yeah. Huh. Well, I hope it can be sanitized." Actually that was fairly cool. The tiles looked like river stone and wood, which had a rustic, I-have-a-sauna kind of look. "Tell him it's fine. Very relaxing."

He didn't even roll his eyes. Much.

"I will." Shuffling close, Cullen patted his butt. "Aren't you glad I started dealing with him?"

"It was that or murder, love." He leaned over, stole a kiss. "Don't forget we have reservations for supper. You promised I could watch you eat cannoli."

"Uhn." Cullen licked Matt's lower lip. "Pasta. Mascarpone. I'm in."

"That's for after, love. The cannoli is foreplay."

Cullen laughed out loud, the sound natural and happy and perfect. "Yeah? I'm good at all the parts, or so you tell me."

"I tell you what, there's something to be said for hooking up with an athlete." Thank God for stamina and really good lubrication.

"And it's not the snowboarding lessons, right?"

Matt chuckled. "I may never get any better at that." He'd done the pipe over the winter. Once. Still, it was more fun than golf. Way more speed involved.

"So, you can sign the work order as finished for Nev," Cullen told him. "I'll get the crew to install the TV."

"Right." He signed off on the project, then looked around. "Doesn't even look like my old place."

"Nope. I wouldn't let bargain basement guests stay in your old place."

Oh, asshole. It had been very dorm room, though. Their newly renovated place in Ben's old apartment was so much better. They had kept Matt's bed.

"You're just missing my futon."

"Never mention it again." Matt's phone beeped and Cullen snorted. "See you at five thirty."

"Wear the gray shirt. I like it best."

"You got it, babe." Cullen patted his ass again before turning away so he could answer his phone.

There was a snafu with one of the service elevators, and there were four different conventions wanting to book for October.

Excellent.

Matt waved to his partner and checked the hallway before running for the service stairs. He had a dinner date, so he'd better get his ass to work.

# *Coming in January 2017*

## ⊚REAMSPUN DESIRES

#25

**The Virgin Manny** by Amy Lane

Growing up and falling in love...

Sometimes family is a blessing and a curse. When Tino Robbins is roped into helping his sister deliver premade dinners when he should be studying for finals, he's pretty sure it's the latter! But one delivery might change everything.

Channing Lowell's charmed life changes when his sister dies and leaves him her seven-year-old son. He's committed to doing what's best for Sammy... but he's going to need a lot of help. When Tino lands on his porch, Channing is determined to recruit him to Team Sammy.

Tino plans to make his education count—even if that means avoiding a relationship—but as he falls harder and harder for his boss, he starts to wonder: Does he have to leave his newly forged family behind in order live his promising tomorrow?

#26

**Extrasensual Perception** by Rayna Vause

If a stalker doesn't kill them, the heat between them might.

Christopher Vincent is desperate enough for a job that he accepts an offer to entertain as a psychic in a friend's nightclub. Jackson Whitman, the club's other owner, is less then thrilled by the new act. To him, psychics are ridiculous and a liability. But when they come face-to-face, attraction flares to life between them.

Someone is watching Jack and Chris from the shadows. What starts as a series of creepy encounters leads to deadly attacks.

Jack and Chris must set aside their differences and work together to survive a homicidal stalker. But can they survive their explosive connection?

## *Now Available*

#21

**Romancing the Wrong Twin** by Clare London

How tangled can a romantic web get?

When gruff mountaineer Dominic Hartington-George seeks sponsorship for his latest expedition, his London PA insists on a more media-friendly profile—like dating celebrity supermodel Zeb Z.

Zeb can't make the date, so he asks his identical twin, Aidan, to stand in for just one evening. Aidan, a struggling playwright, shuns the limelight to the extent people don't even know Zeb has a sibling, but he reluctantly agrees.

When the deception has to continue beyond the first date, Aidan fights to keep up the pretense. Dominic likes his sassy, intelligent companion, and Aidan starts falling for the forthright explorer. But how long can Aidan's conscience cope as confusion abounds? Will coming clean as "the other twin" destroy the trust they've built?

#22

**Seven-Card Stud** by Ava Drake

Temptation, peril, and dirty poker.

Love is a high-stakes game.

When Collin Callahan, British secret agent, goes up against math genius turned surfer bum Oliver Elliot, the battle is epic—and so is the attraction. They're pitted against each other in an exclusive, ultra-secret—and ultra-illegal—poker match in Gibraltar, but when players start dying and they could be next, they find a common goal: catch the killer before it's too late.

Evenly matched at poker and romance, they each wrestle personal demons that threaten to consume them as the stakes climb. It's an all or nothing gamble with both life and love on the line as they fight to be the last seven-card studs standing.

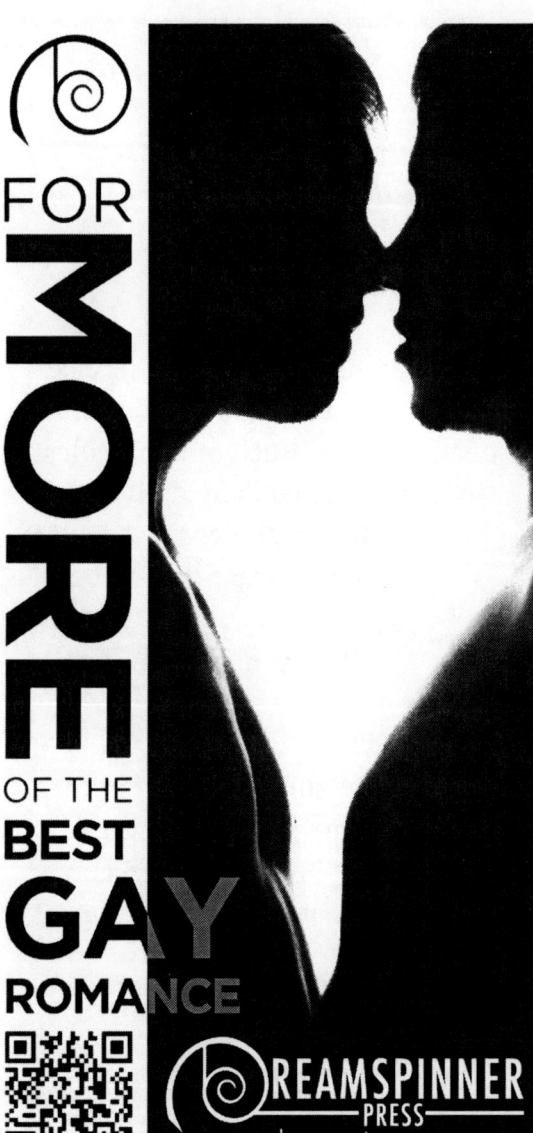